I0539181

Blaster Squad #6

Galaxy of Evil

By

Russ Crossley

53RD STREET PUBLISHING

Published by 53rd Street Publishing
Offices in Gibsons, B.C. Canada and Lincoln City
Oregon, U.S.A

Blaster Squad #6
Galaxy of Evil

Published by 53rd Street Publishing

Copyright © 2018 Russ Crossley

Cover art © SpinningAngel/53rdstreetpublishing

Cover designed by R. Edgewood
Cover design and layout © 2018 by 53rd Street Publishing
Print ISBN: 978-1-927621-59-2

53rd Street Publishing
Head office: Gibsons B.C. Canada
www.53rdstreetpublishing.com

Blaster Squad Series

Acknowledgements

Thank you to my family and friends for your love and support this past year. Truly the best of times and the worst of times.

Dedication

For Glenn, my son and my friend, I think of you
every day. Love you forever.

Introduction

It is nearing a year since the sudden and unexpected passing of our beloved son, Glenn, and I am still in mourning not only for his loss to this world but for the loss of his talent and potential to make our world a better place.

Glenn was a talented actor, producer, and playwright who was on the verge of breaking out. He was finally being financially and spiritually rewarded for his hard work and dedication to his craft. His mother and I have always been proud of him and supportive of his passions and would have done anything to help him.

He had reached the age of thirty and had blossomed into a caring and compassionate man as we always hoped he would. His friends spoke so highly of him and how knowing him made their lives better. To us this speaks volumes about the man he became.

Glenn, wherever you are please know I love you from the depths of my being and will never forget how you made me a better person.

Thank you, son.

Russ Crossley
Gibsons, B.C.
February 2018

1

Berlin, European-Asian Confederation
Earth
Sol system
4141.6.24 Galactic

ALFONSO RIPE ADJUSTED the weapons belt around
his waist to balance the weight of the heavy blaster
on his right hip with the six extra charge cartridges
for his pistol. Coupled with the various pouches
containing equipment he might need, the belt was
designed to support a considerable amount of weight.
Not that his muscular frame couldn't handle it, but
when the belt was out of balance, it could be very
uncomfortable.

In his right hand he held the palm-sized
transmitter linked to the shielded ghost explosive
devices he had planted over the last week throughout
the house and grounds of Syd Bonetes' five-thousand-
hectare estate.

Blaster Squad #6 Galaxy of Evil

The pool house, the ten guest houses, the groundskeeper's residence set amongst the multicolored ancient azaleas and rhododendrons scattered across the grounds, and the hover car garage with its collection of five hundred and fifty-seven shiny antique hover cars were all set to go out in a blaze of fire and death.

Alfonso's ink-black eyes scanned the green, grassy lawn that led to the more than one-hundred-bedroom mansion beyond the nest of pine trees and squat bushes where he stood ready to watch the mayhem that he was about to unleash. The bushes and trees provided him cover from the security patrols by both the human, not so human, and robotic private guard force protecting Bonetes from his long list of enemies. What Bonetes and his security director hadn't anticipated was an inside man like Alfonso Ripe.

His employer, Asia Call, had recruited Alfonso during his first year at the Alliance Naval Academy, enticing him with a promise to train him as a covert operative and explosives expert and to pay him enough credits to build his own life separate from his father's web of lies and crime. That was two years ago. Today was his graduation.

Alfonso's eyes dropped to the device in his hand. His stomach muscles tightened and beads of sweat formed on his forehead. Syd had just arrived home from his suborbital flight from Paris. He didn't like materializers, preferring to get around the old-fashioned way. Of course, a man as rich as Syd didn't take a commercial flight; he owned a fleet of spacecraft and suborbital ships for his and his corporate executives' use.

Commercial flight was for people and aliens at the lower end of the pay scale, or as Syd often joked in private, the sheep he so easily fleeced.

Syd Bonetes also had a variety of business operations on numerous worlds throughout the galaxy, some legal, some borderline legal, and some definitely illegal.

Over sixty years ago, Syd *legally* stole a revolutionary gravity compensator technology for starships—from a scientist who knew nothing about trademarks and copyrights—that Syd eventually sold for more than five trillion credits for which he received the highest civilian award for innovation from the Alliance Council. Since then he had started several food and water distribution companies that quickly grew to multitrillion-credit success stories.

He had eventually become the richest human in the Alliance.

Of course, this distribution system also provided the perfect conduit for one of his most profitable illegal endeavors, arms dealing. For Syd, everything was about profit; people didn't matter, the exception being his family.

Now someone was determined he and his family should be eliminated. Who it was or why was above Alfonso's pay grade, his only job was to fulfill the contract to make sure Syd Bonetes and all of his clan were dead.

Alfonso's covert mission had begun when he was hired to conduct a security threat assessment by Syd's security director. He then spent the next sixteen weeks learning the layout of the grounds and the houses and all he could about Syd's habits and his schedule.

Alfonso closed his eyes and pictured the smiling, round, tanned features of the trillionaire who was joining his extended family for a birthday celebration for his grandchild Eloise, a precocious ten year old, the third child of his daughter Mai. The birthday celebration was the ideal time to take out Syd and his family. Only Alfonso wasn't sure he could do it.

He was uncertain if he could murder these people, including fifty house staff who were about to die because they were in the wrong place at the wrong time working for the wrong arms dealer.

The strains of classical music echoed across the grounds, snapping him back to reality. He opened his eyes and froze as he heard the sounds of footsteps close by, muffled by the grass. Nearby the branches of the surrounding trees rustled in the quiet night as a breath of wind washed over him carrying with it the scent of fresh cut grass and evergreen trees.

Dropping to his haunches, Alfonso sucked in a breath. His eyes flitted left, then right, searching for any signs of movement. He stuffed the remote detonator in his nylon jacket's pocket and reached for the stiletto in a sheath strapped to his right calf. He slowly withdrew it, then held the razor-sharp knife ready to strike if the footsteps came too close. He didn't want to alert the guard post by using his blasters. Slitting a prey's throat was much quieter.

"Anything?" said a feminine voice from behind and to his left.

"Nah," came a reply from a male he thought was slightly to the first voice's right. "This scanner's a piece of junk." Alfonso heard a slap of flesh to metal.

"This thing shows images that might be human, then they disappear every time I take a couple of steps." The male snorted in disgust. "Everything they give us is navy surplus garbage. No wonder the military unloaded this crap."

There was a brief rustling, then the voices and the footsteps began to fade into the distance. Alfonso never saw them but the guards had obviously begun to move away from his hiding place. He gradually released the breath he'd been holding and slipped the knife back in the sheath, then rose to standing once again. His hand slipped into the pocket of his jacket where his fingers embraced the cool metallic feel of the detonator. *I have to decide*, he mused.

A sense of calm came over him as he mulled over his options, then made up his mind. He stepped out of the cover of the bushes and headed for the front entrance to the mansion. Suddenly a deep male voice instructed him to stop where he was and a bright spotlight fell over him.

He froze. "It's me. Alfonso Ripe," he called, his voice echoing over the estate.

Two armed guards appeared from the security office near the front entrance rushing toward him. They each held a blaster pistol at the ready.

One was a foot taller than the other but both wore body armor and helmets with tinted faceplates. They quickly moved to flanking positions and the leader of the duo signaled with his free hand for Alfonso to accompany them to the security office.

Though he couldn't see their faces—in particular their eyes—Alfonso knew they'd shoot him without flinching if he made any move to draw a weapon. Consequently he kept his arms hanging loosely at his sides.

"I have information about a threat—" Alfonso began to say before the shorter of the two guards cut him off.

"No talking," ordered a husky female voice.

Alfonso shrugged and started walking, the two guards a few paces behind. When he arrived at the door to the office, he saw Security Director Pali Kekseo, a former captain in the Hetov system's defense league navy, who had hired him for this assignment. Kekseo was a humorless alien who had limited patience and was constantly suspicious of everyone around him. He had been known to remove key members of his staff for the smallest of infractions yet tolerate those who stole or hid their corrupt behavior, such as accepting bribes, from him.

He was an enigma and unpredictable, which made him very dangerous.

The slate gray-faced Kekseo looked up from an information data pad he'd been reading from as Alfonso entered. His long blond hair-covered fingers grasped his reading glasses, which he took off to set on the desk next to the data pad as he eased back in the leather executive chair. He regarded Alfonso as if he were a rodent.

With saying a word, he stood and nodded to the two guards who had escorted Alfonso into the office to leave them. They closed the door behind them leaving Alfonso alone with the director.

"Please sit," the director said indicating an empty chair across the desk from him. Kekseo's voice had the musical quality common to Hetovians.

Alfonso was secretly pleased they hadn't removed his weapons. He sat and regarded the director with his best imitation of puzzlement. "Is there a problem, Director?"

A corner of Kekseo's mouth curled upward, and his mint green pupils flared briefly as he sat down once again. His steady gaze never left Alfonso. Alfonso detected the faint orange scent of Okol tea in the air.

The director didn't drink tea, but he knew who did. Asty Bonetes, Syd's oldest son and right hand in his business empire. He must have been here a short while ago. The question was why? Asty rarely spent time dealing with security matters.

Alfonso's right hand dropped to rest on the butt of the blaster secured in the holster. Something didn't feel right.

"Of course not, Kid," Kekseo said with a shrug.

The Director had taken to calling him the kid ever since he was hired. It might have been because Alfonso was too unimportant for Kekseo to know his real name or it might be an insult due to his youthful appearance. Not that it mattered because Alfonso didn't mind the moniker.

"Then how can I help you, sir?"

Kekseo's eyes drifted away toward the unadorned beige wall behind him. "You said you had information about a threat?"

"Yes, sir. I was doing a routine recon of the grounds and discovered a number of explosive devices planted around the buildings, including the main house." His eyes surveyed the office. "A few are even planted near the security office."

Kekseo arched one pale blond eyebrow but otherwise showed very little reaction to this information. "Oh, really?" His eyes narrowed. "Interesting." He paused and Alfonso gripped the butt of his blaster pistol tighter.

Finally the director snorted derisively. "You seem to know a lot about the location of these devices, as you call them." His cold stare fell on Alfonso. "I think *you* planted them."

Alfonso considered his options. Pull his pistols and raise the alarm, or deny the accusation and try to delay his impending capture, which appeared inevitable. Kekseo had a well-known reputation for torture to extract information before a summary execution. Over the millennia torture had been proven ineffective, but that fact didn't seem in any way to limit the security director's use of it. Alfonso decided a good offense was preferable to a questionable defense when the outcome didn't seem to be in doubt. He pulled his pistols and leveled them at the Director.

Kekseo offered him a tight, humorless grin. There was no trace of fear or concern in his eyes.

Alfonso's stomach muscles tightened. He pressed the firing stud on the blaster in his right hand. Nothing happened. "A blaster neutralizer," he said in a low voice.

"Yes, Kid. Drop those blasters." Alfonso loosened his grip until the blasters clattered to the floor. Kekseo stood. "Kid, we have to—" His words were cut short, his eyes wide, staring at the hilt of the knife buried in the center of his chest.

"Sorry, did I interrupt you?" asked Alfonso.

Kekseo emitted a tortured gurgle as he sagged forward, then dropped facedown across the desk. There was very little blood, indicating Alfonso had run the blade through the director's heart.

Alfonso dropped to his haunches, grabbed his pistols, and shoved them into their holsters. He stood, then rolled the director over onto his back. The Hetovian's sightless eyes stared at the ceiling. Alfonso gripped the knife and grunted due to the exertion of extracting the knife from the dead alien's chest. After pausing to wipe the bloodstained blade on Kekseo's uniform tunic, Alfonso slipped the knife into the sheath on his calf under his pant leg.

Scanning the desk, he saw the data pad the director had been reading when he came in and picked it up. It had to have an icon to deactivate the neutralizer. There were twenty or so icons on the pad but he wasn't sure which one would deactivate the device.

11

His eyes narrowed. Placing the pad on the desk again, he took out a five-millimeter-long metallic tube he kept on his weapons belt. He unscrewed the top to reveal a fine powder comprised of metal shavings he used to mark spots with traces of dust that a portable scanner could detect so he wouldn't get lost. Only this time he would use the fine powder for something very different than he ever anticipated.

He shook some of the powder across the data pad's screen, then pulled out his portable scanner from a pouch on his belt. Counting to five before he ran the scanner, he detected a slight temperature variation in the fine powder over one icon. Placing the scanner back in the pouch, he held his breath as he pressed his index finger on the icon. It briefly changed color from yellow to purple, then back again to yellow.

He hoped the temperature variation was due to the director's body heat when he pressed it to activate the blaster neutralizer. Pulling one blaster pistol from its holster, Alfonso set it on the lowest setting, aimed at a holo-image of a brown dog-like creature on the desk, then depressed the firing stud. A beam from the blaster enveloped the holo-image until it disappeared. Satisfied the blaster was once again active, he reset the pistol to heavy stun, then reholstered it.

He sucked in a breath to steady his nerves and considered his next steps. He would stun the guards outside this office, then make his way into the mansion and kill Syd and his oldest son. He wasn't about to kill anyone else. He wasn't about to have innocent blood on his hands.

Moving to the closed door, he took out one blaster and counted to five, then kicked the door open and fired.

2

Seattle, North American Protectorate
Earth
Sol system
4154.1.26 Galactic

Thirteen Years Later...

NICK JUSTICE SET the disposable cup on the plasti-steel table and sighed. The warm, milky coffee in his mouth had suddenly lost its smoky, slightly sweet flavor. His sky-blue eyes drifted toward the floor to ceiling windows displaying the expanse of sun-kissed blue-green ocean stretching out toward the thin haze of cloud in the far distance.

Seated across the table from him was Alliance Council Chairman, and President and CEO of Terraform Incorporated, Edgar Whizzar. The chairman's dark eyes were grim, and dark circles had formed under his lower eyelids. His ink-black hair now had streaks of gray running through it. The stress of the past year and a half had taken a toll on the man.

"How bad are we talking?" Nick asked, keeping his voice low so as not to attract attention in the busy coffee shop of the Northwest Regional Alliance headquarters building. The hum of conversation around them masked their conversation and meant anyone clandestinely recording them would have greater difficulty. Given what they knew of the Master, there were probably spies everywhere.

"We've lost contact with fifty-three worlds near the border with the badlands. And so far, sixty-seven starships have failed to report in at their assigned dates and times."

Whizzar grunted, then lifted the coffee cup to his lips and took a sip. After setting the cup back on the gray-and-white marble table, he continued. "Some of our best captains were on those missing ships, and forty-three of the planets that aren't responding to our communications produce significant quantities of the drive plasma necessary to fuel our fleets. I am *very* worried," he added lastly.

Nick arched an eyebrow. "Reserves?"

Whizzar avoided Nick's gaze. He shook his head. "Eight months, maybe a little more. After that we won't have enough drive plasma to intercept an attack before the enemy arrives in an Alliance controlled system."

"What about nuclear fuel for sublight engines?"

Whizzar shrugged. "Yes, we have plenty of nuclear fuel for the fleet; but without new sources of drive plasma, every Alliance world will soon be confined within their home systems." His world-weary gaze locked with Nick's. "And you know what that means."

Nick nodded grimly. "The enemy will drop into any Alliance controlled system using their FTL drive, resulting in a time-space displacement wave that will guarantee the system will be destroyed. Billions of lives and the survival of the Alliance rest on us being able to intercept the enemy fleet as far as possible from inhabited Alliance planets."

"Either that or we surrender." He snorted derisively. "I'm certain the Master would *love* conquering the Alliance without firing a shot—"

Nick's jaw tightened. "I, for one, am not going to let that happen." His eyes shifted to look out the window, then back to Whizzar's gray features and sunken cheeks. The threat of war over the past year and a half had weighed heavily on the man.

"Neither am I," said Whizzar. The chairman's bloodshot eyes narrowed. "Why didn't you engage your FTL drive in the Theta Pergonae system?

"You could have destroyed their fleet, stopping them in their tracks."

Nick thought back to the massive green-blue world covered mostly by water. Theta Pergonae IV, also known by its Alliance code name, Poseidon. Over these past months since rescuing the Kid and Siren, he'd had a chance to conduct an extensive review of the sensor data collected by the experimental starship *Lightning* during the mission. There was another M class planet in the system, which would have also been placed at risk of being destroyed along with any life on its surface if they had engaged the FTL drive.

"Our FTL drive would not engage within the system. There was too much electromagnetic interference and high levels of ion radiation to maintain a time-displacement field." His jaw stiffened. "Besides the fact that even if I could have engaged the drive, I wouldn't have. I don't kill innocents. You know this, Edgar." Without realizing it, Nick had raised his voice and a number of heads had turned in their direction.

Glancing at the tables nearest them, he offered the other guests a tight, humorless smile. They each in turn looked away and went back to their own conversations.

He then lowered his voice, leaned forward slightly in his chair, and continued. "I have Gears working on a few ideas that might offer some hope of success."

"What are they?" Whizzar asked, his eyes brimming with interest.

The sides of Nick's mouth curled slightly and his eyes narrowed. "My brilliant tech genius has more than a few frauds up his wrappers." *Wrappers? Or do I mean sleeves? I'm not sure.*

Whizzar eyed him skeptically as a mirthless smile played across his lips. "I sometimes have no idea what you're talking about; however it's clear enough that the upgrades to the *Lightning* are proceeding well."

Nick nodded. *Siren tells me I mangle my granddad's sayings but at least the chairman understood my meaning.* Gears had added defensive screens, including a stealth shield, and more powerful blaster cannons though he wasn't able to increase the size of the plasma fuel tank without compromising hull integrity. There just wasn't any additional space to be had.

Simulations showed that under FTL flight, an increase in hull size would rupture with a larger plasma fuel tank.

18

Of course this meant humanoid passengers would be vaporized in the resulting explosion. Obviously killing your crew wasn't the most desired outcome. Without significant redesign, the engineers concluded the ESS *Lightning* could still only carry enough fuel for a one-way trip. So far they hadn't discovered the balance between hull design and the new FTL engine design that would alleviate the problem.

Locating fuel at the other end had worked out on their trip to Poseidon, but it might not be so conveniently nearby next time. Of course the chairman knew all these facts but Gears was also working on some very special enhancements he'd only told Nick about.

The chairman glanced around them to ensure no one was paying them too much attention, then leaned toward him. "I have something special to show you."

Nick arched one eyebrow. *Intriguing.* "Lead on, sir."

3

Seattle, North American Protectorate
Alliance Headquarters
Earth
Sol system
4154.1.26 Galactic

NICK FOLLOWED THE chairman into his office on
the top floor of the Alliance headquarters building,
past the Estuian administrative assistant whose name
he couldn't recall seated at the workstation nearest
the door. To him she looked more like a guard than
an admin assistant. Given her muscular arms and
severe watchful gaze as she studied him, it wouldn't
surprise him if she had a blaster ready under the desk
to take him out if he made a move she didn't like. The
chairman hadn't been popular with more than a few
planets in Alliance space even before the threat of
the Master had added an even more urgent need for
additional security precautions.

The utilitarian, carpeted office was large with
floor to ceiling windows made of smoked translucent
plasti-glass through which Nick could see Lake
Washington in the distance.

The sun-kissed blue water was covered in small whitecaps created by the light winds. This time of year the air and water were warm so the surface of the lakes was dotted with numerous sails of boats.

The chairman moved toward the expansive onyx-colored desk in a black leather executive chair. There were five wide comfortable chairs in front of the desk, and to the left were chairs sufficient to seat twenty-five humans and aliens surrounding a long oak board table that had to be six meters in length. The walls were adorned by framed paintings that depicted artist's impressions of a variety of worlds from across the Alliance, including the fire world of Ember IV and the kilometers-high waterfalls on Telus II.

"Please sit," said the chairman as he sat in the leather executive chair behind his desk. Nick selected one of the five wide leather chairs in front of the chairman's desk and sat down.

The chairman leaned back, his gaze directed at the board table. "SIN, bring up the briefing screen."

So the chairman had his own System Information Network artificial intelligence installed in his office. Interesting. And expensive. Nick watched a tri-screen appear from a hidden section in the center of the board table.

A section of the table seemed to melt away to allow the screens to appear from within and there was no sound as it locked into place. Something his grandfather once said popped into Nick's mind. *Spare no expensive credits.* Or something like that.

The screens came to life, depicting an image Nick assumed was a space shipyard with a spacecraft of a design type he had never seen before. His brow wrinkled. It wasn't the Armstrong Shipyard orbiting Earth where Gears was right now making the final adjustments to the *Lightning's* upgrades. He shifted his gaze to Whizzar. "What is that?"

Whizzar eased back in the chair and steepled his hands in front of him. One corner of his mouth curled while his eyes became hard. "I named it the ESS *Thunder*." Whizzar swiveled his chair toward the wall of smoked glass. "It's the sister ship to the *Lightning*. Same capabilities as the refitted *Lightning*, but with a plasma fuel tank with twice the capacity. I ordered its construction at a top secret facility away from prying eyes and hopefully the Master's spies." He cleared his throat. "I also ordered the *Lightning* be commissioned as an Alliance naval vessel. It's no longer considered an experimental ship."

Nick's stomach tightened and anger boiled from his belly.

His mouth suddenly tasted slightly metallic. Whizzar turned to face him, a grin forming on his lips. "Before you say anything, I also ordered the *Lightning* be loaned to Blaster Squad for the duration of the emergency."

Nick swallowed his anger. "So we won't be reporting to the navy?" Edgar Whizzar knew the last thing Nick would accept was his squad of mercenaries being tethered to the navy. There was no way he would accept such an arrangement even if his crew agreed to something so outrageous, which he knew none of them would. He had left the navy for good reasons and he wasn't about to be ordered around by one of their self-important strutting-like-a-peacock admirals.

The wry grin on Whizzar's rugged features faded. "You can take that to the bank. You're free to do what you think is right…provided you don't interfere with naval operations."

Nick eyed the chairman with one eyebrow arched. "Okay, with the proviso that no one except me decides if any action *I* deem necessary goes too far. No discussion, no court of appeal."

The chairman avoided him by swiveling the chair to face the window again. He looked thoughtful before responding.

"Okay, Nick, I know you're a man of principal." He shrugged. "My admirals won't like it once the situation gets sticky—which it will—but I'll make sure my standing orders are very clear regarding you and your merry band of mercenaries." He looked back at Nick over his right shoulder with an amused glint in his eyes. "Agreed?"

Nick didn't see any sign of deception in the chairman's eyes or in his body language. "Agreed."

Whizzar abruptly stood. "If that's all for now, I have a few more meetings today before I head back to Alliance headquarters."

Nick rose to his feet. "When will the *Thunder* be ready?"

Whizzar shrugged. "It's ready now. You'll find it at the Armstrong shipyard later today."

Whizzar lead the way to the door to the outer office. They paused before the door opened. Whizzar locked eyes with Nick. "You will pick the crew from your squad for the *Thunder*. People you trust." His jawline tightened, suggesting to Nick this decision hadn't been easy to get past his admirals. "No one will overrule your decisions. I've seen to that."

Nick nodded just as the door slid aside to reveal the outer office where the administrative assistant sat at the workstation, her almond-shaped eyes focused on a monitor on the desk. Her eyes flitted to them as they exited the chairman's office together.

Nick came up short when he saw who was seated in the waiting area on a three-meter couch against the far wall. Grand Admiral of the Alliance Navy, Hiram Costello, and his aide-de-camp, Commodore Tozeth, regarded him through narrow, angry eyes. Nick nodded to the two senior naval officers, then looked back at Whizzar. "Thank you, Edgar. I'll be in touch before we leave orbit."

Whizzar nodded, then beckoned the two senior naval officers to follow him into his office with a wave of his right hand. The three beings disappeared behind the door as it slid closed.

Nick released the breath he'd been holding, and the stomach muscles he hadn't realized were knotted tight finally relaxed. *If this keeps up, I'm gonna get ulcers.*

Nick had to transport to the Armstrong shipyard in orbit as soon as possible and find Gears and the other members of Blaster Squad. He wanted to get underway in two days. They needed to find out what was happening at the Alliance frontier.

He stood in front of the bank of lift cars waiting for one to stop on this floor. His foot tapped involuntarily.

He couldn't wait to get to his ship.

A loud explosion followed by a blast wave thudded over him causing his hearing to suddenly disappear. The floor under him shifted violently, causing him to lose his balance. He landed on his side as if he'd been knocked over by a high wind. There hadn't been an earthquake in this area for more than a thousand years, and planetary engineers had ensured there never would be one again.

The carpeted floor beneath him trembled powerfully and the overhead lighting flickered once, then went out. He thought he could hear the ghosts of screams and the groaning of overstressed steel carried on the swirling wind but the sounds were muffled as if he were underwater. The windows facing the lake behind him in the reception area provided enough light so he could still see though his vision was partially obscured by the billowing, acrid smoke.

Waving away the smoke, he peered through the shadowy haze back toward the administrative assistant's workstation and saw she was gone and a large section of the building with her. The carpet had been shredded and the torn threads of material waved in the fierce wind. The chairman's office was located on the fortieth floor where the winds were stronger than at ground level.

He coughed, his heart beating rapidly in his chest, his lips and throat dry. *What the hell am I seeing?*

Beyond the reception, where the chairman's office had been, was empty air. The office was gone, meaning so were Edgar Whizzar and Grand Admiral Costello.

As the realization of what had just happened swept over him, Nick's gut tightened again and his mouth tasted coppery metallic. This wasn't a natural disaster, it was an assassination; and he knew immediately who was behind it.

4

ANSS Lightning
Armstrong Shipyard
Earth orbit
Sol system
4154.2.19 Galactic

Nick sat in the now familiar copilot's seat next to Gears, seated at the pilot's seat. The flight deck of the *Lightning* wasn't as spacious as the *Hunter,* but since they needed to get to the frontier as soon possible and this was the faster ship, it was the spacecraft they required for the moment.

Nick brought the mug of warm, milky coffee to his lips and took a generous sip. The liquid flowed over his tongue and down his throat, enveloping him in a sense of comfort. "So what do you think, Gears?"

The tech genius glanced at him and smirked. "Oh, we've been good to go for a couple of weeks as you well know, Captain."

"Okay, then let's boot this pig in the bottom and get the show on the space lane."

Gears chuckled and shook his head at Nick no doubt mangling of one of his grandfather's sayings. He'd known Nick for so many years that he'd heard just about every variation of this catalogue of cultural nonsense from millennia past. Put simply, he was used to his commanding officer's whimsical side. "I'll signal the *Thunder* we're about to leave the shipyard." Gears drained his mug followed by a loud, theatrical swallow. "Finally," he added, eliciting a glare of mock derision from Nick.

It had been twenty-four days since the assassination of Edgar Whizzar by the Master's agents, and the ensuing chaos had delayed their departure.

Alliance Council Vice Chairwoman Lokfor Ust, an Estuian and President and CEO of Holo Systems Communications, was appointed chair of the Alliance Council in a unanimous vote. No one on the council appeared eager to oppose her appointment. As the second in command to Whizzar, it made sense she be elevated to the late chairman's position.

After assuming her post as vice chairwoman a decade ago, Ust preferred to go by the first name of Lucille to appear more palatable to Earthers since she now resided amongst humans on the home world of the Alliance.

She was a self-described hard, emotionless, and highly driven executive who took no figurative prisoners, always aiming for excellence in everything she touched. She was also renown as being the toughest negotiator in the galaxy. As a close friend of Asia Call—rumors were they were closer than blood relatives—she too often complicated Nick's life further than he would have liked. She frequently objected to Chairman Whizzar's support for Nick and Blaster Squad.

Chairwoman Ust promoted Admiral Bellot Schipp to Grand Admiral in command of the Alliance Navy. Rumor was there were those on the council who didn't want Schipp for the top post, saying he was too much of a hothead; but what Ust wants, she gets. Schipp and Nick had history—some would call it baggage—which meant in that single attack Nick had lost two of his closest allies at the highest level of the Alliance. Not that Grand Admiral Costello had always been a supporter of Blaster Squad, but Edgar had managed to convince the naval officer of the usefulness of Nick and his mercenaries on more than a few occasions.

Chairwoman Ust also promoted Al-Mok Talon, head of Alliance Security, to Vice Chair of the council.

Promoting someone to second-in-command from outside the sitting council members was unprecedented in the long history of the Alliance, but since they were on a war footing, not entirely unexpected. The Alliance had never faced a threat like the one posed by the Master, whose ambition was to replace the council with himself as Emperor.

Talon had personally conducted the interrogations of Commander Caddowth, Sonara's doppelganger, and the traitorous Xeyrian, Stuat'ir. Blaster Squad had captured this cadre of traitors during their last mission to the planet Poseidon. When Nick enquired about the prisoners six months ago after hearing nothing more about them since they were turned over to Alliance Security, he was told they were *missing*. Missing being the euphemism for certain death. He wouldn't see them again, that much was certain.

Alliance Security was known to eliminate prisoners after they extracted the information they needed. It was considered efficient and didn't leave anyone around to talk about AS's methodology so they couldn't be prosecuted for any illegalities that may have occurred in the course of the interrogation.

Torture had long been officially illegal under Alliance law, but there continued to be ugly rumors about torture and the use of banned mind-altering drugs to extract information. There were also unconfirmed rumors about a device from an unaligned planet, used to drain subject's memories, leaving them an empty husk.

Nick continued to be curious concerning the information Talon extracted that he wasn't going to be privy to until he was en route to the rim worlds. Or at least those were the instructions he'd received along with the encrypted orders Talon transmitted to the *Lightning*'s SIN two days ago.

The encryption code to open the files would be transmitted to them once they passed through the Alliance Defense Grid at the outer edge of Earth's solar system. Nick thought about asking Gears to break into the files anyway, but after considering the possible consequences if Talon discovered what he'd done, he decided to wait. Talon didn't know the meaning of the words *forgiveness* or *mistake,* so though Nick was good at selling his intentional *mistakes,* Talon would order him executed regardless, and probably Gears too for helping the mistake occur. No, these were dangerous times and not just because of the impending war.

The balance of power in the galaxy was shifting, and not in the direction of freedom and human and alien rights.

Pushing aside his uncertainties, Nick turned to look at Bones at the weapons station and smiled to himself. "You enjoying the new toys, big guy?" The refit to the *Lightning* included two three-barrel batteries of high yield blaster cannons and two missile launchers with a large supply of missile types from stealth to standard plasma. There was also a small supply of the newly developed FTL-capable missiles that could be launched within a planetary system with minimal disruption to the system's planets and other space bodies. The wide-eyed wonder and boyish grin on Bones' rugged features made him look like a kid in a candy store on his birthday. He was clearly very excited about the new weapons.

"You better believe it, boss. I can't wait to try these babies out in action."

Nick wanted to avoid the use of these weapons on this mission, but it was better to be heavily armed that not. Ust assured him before they left for the shipyard that the mission would be surveillance and report only. She said there was no need to attack anyone and possibly die. The Alliance needed information, not martyrs.

They already had too many martyrs as it stood in this clandestine war against the Master's forces.

Nick hoped the newly assigned crewmembers would fit in with Bones and Gears. Mars-born Harry Stacks worked the comm system and Mins Clobe, an Estuian, sat at the sensor station prepping the sensitive instruments for departure. Both beings checked out as far as Nick could ascertain from his sources at Alliance Intelligence and his more underground sources in the tight-knit mercenary community.

Both were experts with blasters and knives, and Clobe was proficient with explosives. It would take time for Nick to trust these two but they both had been freelance mercenaries before joining the Alliance Covert Security Directorate after their respective teams were killed in skirmishes with pirates in the badlands. Of course Nick still had a few friends Talon didn't know about inside ACSD, who provided him additional background on these two after they were recruited. So far they seemed okay. Only time would tell.

"*Thunder* confirms they are ready when we are, Captain," reported Stacks.

"We have approval from traffic control. We are cleared to proceed," added Gears.

"Take us out," Nick said.

A slight pressure on his wide chest told Nick Gears had activated the navigation thrusters. He looked at the middle screen on his station in time to see the massive doors of the repair bay retracting to create a window to Earth orbit beyond. The inky black star-strewn space grew gradually larger with each passing second as the ship gathered momentum. His heart seemed to skip a beat at the sight of open space. It was always his secret thrill to be back in the vastness of space. Not that the Earth system was exactly open space per se. Earth orbit—like many Alliance worlds' space—was busy with a myriad of traffic orbiting the planet at assigned distances. These ships ranged from traders from across the Alliance to private mining ships, navy vessels of every size and configuration, luxury corporate ships, and private yachts of the wealthy, all jockeying for position to fill the so often mis-described empty space. Space wasn't as empty as it might appear to those who lived and worked in it.

Micrometeoroids, bits of flotsam from ships and spent boosters, and even some rare forms of microscopic life filled space with particles too small for the human eye to see.

Navigation shields took care of these tiny particles so they wouldn't penetrate a spacecraft's hull, but still the myth persisted that the space between the planets and stars was essentially empty.

"Traffic control has provided us a course heading and coordinates to the defense grid—" Gears said as he entered the coordinates into the navigation system.

"—We're projecting three days until we reach those coordinates, sir," finished Stacks.

Gears and Stacks exchanged a look of smug understanding, making Nick vaguely uncomfortable. Gears could work with new team members for years before warming up to them. Gears and the Kid had grown to respect each other but they still weren't what Nick would call friends. These two had only known each other for a few days, yet they were already able to finish each other's sentences and neither seemed offended; in fact, they seemed pleased, even amused.

Weird. Nick made a mental note to follow up later with them both. This strange friendship didn't make much sense given all he knew about Gears. Now he wished he knew more about Stacks than what was in his file.

5

NICK GAZED OVER the rim of his glass of orange
juice at Gears, seated across from him at the mess
table. They were alone, leaving Bones in charge
on the flight deck. Beside Gears sat Siren, looking
worried, her brow furrowed and her eyes narrowed.
She had barely touched her cucumber and tomato
sandwich and the glass of almond milk on the table in
front of her.

Siren had transported to the *Lightning* from the
Thunder so they could discuss their strategy once
they made the FTL jump to their next destination,
identified in the orders they were about to see for the
first time.

"SIN, activate the wall viewer and open file
X7345 dash W," Nick said, rolling his eyes. Secret
codes, clandestine missions. *Ridiculous. This secrecy
crap is one of the reasons I left the navy.*

Just give me my orders and I'll kick butt, take names, and win the battle, thought Nick dismissively.

"I require the second level access code, sir," replied the artificial intelligence.

Nick sighed and scanned the faces of Gears and Siren. When neither of them said anything, he said, "Well? Come on, one of you must have the code."

"Yeah, it's me." Gears shrugged. "SIN, *clockworks.*"

"Second level access code confirmed," replied the AI immediately.

The wall across the mess shimmered, then transformed into a wall-sized monitor displaying an image on the screen that caused Nick to involuntarily suck in a breath. "Edgar Whizzar?"

"Nick Justice and Blaster Squad," the image of the late chairman began, "if you're receiving this message, then I am dead. According to Alliance Intelligence, the Master has been planning to assassinate Grand Admiral Costello and myself for some time now, hoping to weaken the leadership of the Alliance. I can only assume he has succeeded. In concert with Vice Chairwoman Ust and Al-Mok Talon, we have set up a shadow council who will step in should the Master succeed in eliminating us.

This will ensure our attack plans will continue uninterrupted. Of course, this information is beyond top secret."

Nick knew exactly what this classification meant. Revealing any information classified above top secret was the only death penalty statute left on the books.

"Nick," continued the image of Whizzar, "we want you and your team to take *Lightning* and *Thunder* to the outer rim worlds, specifically to Albanel in the Gateway system. Albanel has the largest concentration of plasma fuel ore in the known galaxy and is critical for the success of our campaign to stop the Master's forces." The image of the late chairman paused and his brow furrowed. "We must secure this world for the Alliance before it's too late." The screen went dark.

That's it? How am I supposed to secure an entire planet with two ships? I'm still missing the most critical pieces of this puzzle. Nick wasn't about to go off on some wild turkey chase without all the facts until he was absolutely certain what they'd be facing.

"Stacks, get me Chairwoman Ust. I need to speak with her immediately," Nick said, crossing his arms over his wide chest. Stacks acknowledged saying it would take half an hour for Alliance Command to receive the request, which meant it would take another half hour after that to receive a reply from Ust. A knot of tension formed in the pit of Nick's stomach. Something was making him nervous. He had an uneasy sense time was growing short.

Nick scowled at Siren, who exchanged a look of concern with Gears, standing to her left. "What's wrong, Captain?" asked Gears.

"Siren, tell me about your crew."

Siren arched one eyebrow. She understood immediately. The AIs aboard *Lightning* and *Thunder* shared a surreptitious listening program imbedded within their code. Someone had no doubt imbedded a piece of seemingly random code in the System Information Networks in both vessels to monitor their conversations and transmit them to a person or a place as yet unknown.

Nick also suspected a backup plan of having a spy or two imbedded in either one or both of the ships crews. Stacks and Clobe seemed unlikely candidates. Of course he had initially trusted Commander Caddowth and Siren's sister Sonara, but they had both proved to be expert liars. Without proof any of these new recruits were working against the mission objectives, he couldn't take action. His jaw tightened. But when he did have proof, they'd better not be looking for a way out.

He wasn't in the mood for leniency these days.

They locked eyes as Siren made a slight nod to confirm she understood. "Well, Captain, we recruited three crewmembers from the Fleet Training Academy, they are each top in their respective fields. One is an engineer named Hilo Tiks. He's Lobsan, which means with his four limbs he's quite handy with an engineering panel. He's able to multitask faster than anyone I've ever seen." Her mouth curled at one corner and a flicker of amusement passed over her eyes. "Except, of course, Gears."

The pilot nodded. "Yeah, he's a good kid. I met him when Siren and I went to the academy to check some of the babies out. He seems capable."

Siren continued. "Then we have Posty Mupper, a junior." Nick failed to keep the surprise from his eyes. "Don't worry, Nick. She may be young, but she's incredibly talented with comm gear and sensors. She has something special about her that doesn't seem obvious until you see her in action.

"I witnessed her tear down a perfectly functional comm unit in less than five minutes and rebuild it in twenty to add new features I have never seen before. The instructors were baffled until she showed them how the rebuilt unit could now communicate with Mars and the mining colonies in the outer system.

The experts say what she did is impossible with that class of comm unit. They couldn't explain how she did it." She shrugged. "But the bottom line is, it works."

Siren's eyes shifted to Gears, who had bit off a chunk of his cheese and pickle sandwich and was chewing noisily, then back to Nick. "I went outside the academy for one additional crewmember." She swallowed and avoided his gaze. "Pieter Zoeks." She paused again to take a sip of almond milk from her glass, then continued. "I know you and Zoeks have a past, but he is the most qualified weapons specialist in the Alliance after Bones, and I thought we needed someone highly qualified aboard the *Thunder* in the event we had to make a fight of it."

Nick remembered the Scosi weapons master well. He pictured his brilliant yellow eyes—the color of egg yolks—and the pasty complexion of his square-jawed features. And he remembered the tall, muscular frame that rivaled Bones' strong presence. The biggest difference between the two men was Bones could be outspoken and get ahead of himself by shooting first and asking questions after. In contrast, Zoeks was more thoughtful and wanted to be sure before he started shooting. It was this trait that created the rift with Nick.

Early in his career as a Special Operations Trooper, Nick was on a search and destroy mission with Zoeks in command to put down a rim world rebellion. Nick's best friend, Spenser Lockmind, had been with him when he applied a mine to the door of a building where the enemy was reported to be concentrated. Just before the mine was to explode in the door, Zoeks signaled they were to stand down. He said he had reports of civilians being held hostage inside. When Nick and Spenser began to retreat, the door suddenly burst open and rebel soldiers began firing from within. Spenser was vaporized in the brief firefight.

Normally Nick would have chalked up the experience to the fortunes of war, but after he killed the rebels, he discovered there were no civilians inside. It had been a ruse by the rebels to kill as many Alliance troopers as possible. It was difficult for Nick to forget the incident given he'd had to tell Spenser's new mate about how he died. At least the unclassified version.

Nick's gaze shifted between his two friends. "I trust you two to make the best choices." Siren's shoulders relaxed and Nick realized she had been nervous to tell him she'd hired Zoeks.

He decided to let bygones stay in the past for the good of the mission. He'd enjoy firing Zoeks once they returned. If they returned, of course.

The mission ahead looked to be plenty dangerous and filled with too many unknowns to put his mind at ease.

"Sir." It was Stacks. "We're receiving a message from Alliance Headquarters. It's coded eyes-only for you, Captain."

Nick nodded to Siren and Gears. "Okay, Stacks, I'll take it in my quarters." He stood. "You two get back to your posts. I'll let you know when I'm ready after I decode this message. Regardless, we're going to make the FTL jump so you should start making preparations."

Within ten minutes Nick was seated at the desk in his quarters, staring at the blank screen on the monitor affixed the wall over the desk. His stomach was in knots and his lips were dry. *I wish I'd brought a glass of water from the galley.*

"SIN, voice recognition, Nicholas Justice, Captain, ANSS *Lightning*."

"Confirmed," said the SIN in its mechanical voice.

"Open the transmission from Alliance Headquarters," said Nick, his voice barely above a whisper. The monitor in front of him flashed to life to reveal the familiar image of Sonara Albright. Nick made an involuntary gasp. He had expected it to be a message from Chairwoman Ust.

Sonara wore a sardonic grin on her pale red lips and her dark eyes sparkled with amusement. "Surprised to see me, Nick?" Nick's eyes flicked to the upper right corner of the screen and confirmed the transmission was a recording, not a live message. The knot of tension in his belly relaxed. He sighed and waited for her to continue.

The grin faded and her eyes became serious. "The sneak attack on Chairman Whizzar and the Grand Admiral came from an Alliance Navy ship in Earth orbit. The stealth missile used was designed and built on Albanel. Chairwoman Ust has ordered me to meet your ships in the Gateway system where we are to locate the weapons facility to destroy it, including any stockpile of additional weapons they may have." Her eyes narrowed and her jaw tightened causing a jagged scar that ran across the left side of her chin to pale against her tanned flesh. "And to find those responsible and make sure they never breathe again."

Nick's heart skipped a beat and a burning knot of anger formed in the pit of his stomach. Ust lied to him about the objectives of the mission. And he'd have to cooperate with someone who, as far as he was concerned, was a traitor. Sonara had to be working for the Alliance Covert Security Directorate. He rolled his eyes. But he was eager to avenge the Chairman's murder and he had to do everything in his power to prevent the Master from taking over the Galaxy. It all seemed so frustratingly impossible.

"There are two additional files embedded within the transmission," said the SIN.

"Open them," Nick said, failing to keep the bitterness from his voice. The screen shifted and two documents appeared side by side. Nick began to scan the one on the right and a slow grin spread across his features.

The mission was about to heat up and their chances of survival had just increased by a factor of ten.

6

ANSS Lightning
Fifty-two million kilometers from the Gateway system
4154.3.26 Galactic

NICK'S EYES FLUTTERED open and his vision began to clear almost immediately. Just as he did every time, he concentrated on focusing on a support beam in the ceiling of the FTL pod bay visible through the plasti-steel canopy of the pod. As usual after FTL travel, his stomach felt queasy, as if he were about to vomit any second, but he swallowed hard to counter the stomach-churning effects of the time/space displacement wave. A sharp vibration shot through the cushioned mat he lay on in the FTL stasis pod. He didn't think much about the cause until the intensity of the vibration increased as a second wave of energy came from beneath him.

His sixth sense told him something was very wrong and he better get to the flight deck as soon as possible. "SIN, cycle the canopy open," he said. His throat was dry, his words harsh and raspy.

"It is too soon, Captain. You need another ten minutes recovery time or you will be very ill from the FTL time/space displacement effect."

Nick grunted. *It's as if the SIN has swallowed a user manual.* A sudden sharp shudder shot through the ship forcing him to press his palms flat against the side of the pod to steady himself. Waves of energy shifted the pod sharply left, then right, before the ship once again leveled beneath him. Given the pod was welded to the deck plating, these sudden violent shifts definitely weren't a good sign. The anti-gravity system was struggling to compensate whatever forces were assaulting the ship.

"Forget about the book, SIN," Nick barked, "If I wait ten minutes, you, me, and the rest of the crew will be dead. Understood?"

"Yes, Captain."

The plasti-steel canopy above him cycled open. Nick sucked in a deep breath, gritted his teeth, then slowly began to sit up. Beads of sweat dotted his forehead and dizziness gripped him. Shaking his head to clear his mind, and he used his muscular arms and strong hands to pull himself the rest of the way into a full sitting position. Ignoring the nausea, he dropped his legs over the side of the pod and then to the floor.

Using one hand to push himself off the side of the pod, he stumbled away on rubbery legs toward the lift across the bay. His rational mind told him it was no more than three meters away but it felt like three kilometers. He made it to the lift doors when the deck beneath him rippled and shook violently. To keep from falling, one hand shot out to brace his weight against the wall beside the lift doors. Puffing out his cheeks, he blew the air from his lungs to bury the nausea threatening to overwhelm him. The lift doors hissed opened and he stepped inside as the shuddering stopped.

Closing his eyes, he threw his head back and pressed into the back wall of the lift car. "Flight deck," he murmured under his breath. "SIN, tell me what's happening."

"We are under attack by two unknown vessels. Their configuration suggests decommissioned navy battlewagons. Each is equipped with multiple plasma cannons. So far I have managed to engage the defensive screens milliseconds prior to the first volley and have initiated a standard evasion program. Our defensive screens will not last much longer if we continue to take direct hits."

Nick's eyes flew open when a plate in the ceiling of the lift car slammed into the floor beside him, accompanied by a loud bang.

The lift doors finally opened onto the flight deck. The rush of adrenaline running through Nick's bloodstream cleared his head immediately and he suddenly felt stronger; and his stomach had settled. "Where are the others?" he said as he moved to sit in the copilot's station.

"They have exited the pods and are proceeding to the flight deck," replied the artificial intelligence.

"ETA?"

"They are four point nine seconds from arrival," said the SIN.

Just as SIN said, the lift doors at the rear of the flight deck opened after a few seconds and Clobe, Stacks, Bones, and Gears spilled onto the deck walking to their assigned stations as quickly as they were able on trembling legs. As Gears dropped into the pilot's seat, he glanced at Nick, his face paler than usual. After slipping the bud for the comm system into his left ear, he asked, "Orders, sir?"

"Everyone plugged in?" The response was a chorus of enthusiastic, "Yes, Captain's. "Okay, someone tell me where the *Thunder* is?"

Harry Stacks replied first. "I have Captain Siren on the comm."

But Nick knew he had to deal with the attacking vessels first. "Gears, engage the stealth shield and change course to one nine mark seven three." Nick tried to swallow, but his throat and lips were dry. His stomach churned and he knew he would need an electrolyte drink soon to rebalance his system, but personal comfort was the last thing on his mind at the moment. Survival took precedent over any other considerations.

7

ANSS Lightning
Fifty-two million kilometers from the Gateway system
4154.3.26 Galactic

"BUT, CAPTAIN, THAT heading will set us on a collision course with the attacking vessels," said the SIN. "The stealth shield has failed. They now see us on their sensors. The good news is the defensive screens are still at full power."

Nick coughed to clear his dry throat. He took in a deep breath to focus and to push the discomforting effects of FTL flight from affecting his decision-making from his mind. "Forward defensive screens to full power. Use every bit of power we have to keep those shields at maximum," he said. "Gears, what is *Thunder*'s position?"

"Directly aft of us, Captain."

Nick's eyes narrowed at the middle screen in his station and saw the icon for the *Thunder* was where he needed it to be. *Perfect*. "Good job, Siren," he muttered under his breath.

He realized he had forgotten the comm was still open. "Siren. This is Nick. Take the *Thunder* to the following coordinates in exactly one minute with all weapons at the ready. Forward defense screens on full," he ordered both crews. Nick gave Siren the coordinates he wanted her and her crew to be at when they were ready to fire. *Siren will follow my lead.*

"Understood, Nick." Siren's voice was calm and oozed confidence as it always did no matter how dire the circumstances. "See you in three."

Nick pressed an icon on the screen in front of him and the image shimmered, then solidified to show the two massive, heavily armed ships directly in line with their present heading. He swallowed. It was like looking into the mouth of a volcano, reminding him of the extinct volcanoes he and his grandfather used to hike to when he was a boy. Only the enemy vessels were firing plasma cannons spitting streams of destructive energy across the blackness of space right at them. These two ships were definitely not extinct.

Nick pressed an icon on the screen to his right and it now displayed the heading and velocity information on a simulated graphic. The *Lightning* and the *Thunder* were displayed as flashing green dots, the two enemy vessels as flashing red dots.

The two sets of dots were quickly closing the distance between them.

"SIN, countdown until collision."

"Sir?" replied the SIN, sounding surprised.

"You heard me, Mister."

"Yes, sir. Forty-five seconds, forty-four seconds...." The SIN continued the countdown.

At the thirty second mark, Nick opened the comm to Siren, then shouted, "Siren, break starboard and fire! Gears, break port. Bones, give them everything we've got. All batteries!"

Nick felt the artificial gravity struggling and his stomach seemed to sink as they made the violent course change. His center screen dimmed as the blackness of space lit up with brilliant bursts of energy coming from the *Lightning*'s plasma cannons and blaster batteries being fired in unison.

The two battlewagons on the center screen continued to quickly grow in size as they closed rapidly. The enemy ships' defensive screens were being lit up by the high energy striking them, making them glow. The brightness grew in intensity, getting brighter and brighter as the images of the enemy ships grew ever larger until they filled the screen. Nick changed the magnification as they approached.

Gears had the ship twisting and turning to avoid the enemy ships' weapons fire while Bones expertly fired the *Lightning*'s weapons batteries, making continuous strikes in vital areas of the enemy ships.

Soon the enemy ships' fire began to dwindle as their weapons went off-line. Nick smiled to himself. Siren and Bones had executed the plan perfectly. They'd managed to knock out the weapons power grid, sector by sector, using concentrated fire at key locations in the battlewagons' defensive shields. Good thing these ships were older designs, so the schematics were readily available in the AI's memory core to plan such an attack. Once their weapons were all off-line, the *Lightning* and the *Thunder* would take out the enemy's navigation systems and disable their engines thus leaving the vessels helpless before Nick's ships headed for the planet. It would take time for rescue ships to come to the enemy ships' aid.

Hopefully Blaster Squad would get to Albanel before the Master could rally his forces. From what Nick had been able to determine, overconfidence was the ambitious tyrant's principal weakness. No doubt the Master expected these battlewagons would destroy *Lightning* and *Thunder* before they reached the planet.

What concerned Nick most about these two enemy vessels was they had been waiting here as if they expected an attack in this quadrant of the Gateway system. Someone must have tipped them off about their approach vector. And if that were true, then the mission ahead was likely to be more dangerous than he had anticipated. Then again, since when did Blaster Squad ever face an easy mission?

Regardless, the plan was still a go. Nick's eyes narrowed as he studied the flight graphic. "SIN, are their weapons and engines off-line?"

"Yes, sir."

"Signal *Thunder* we're breaking off our attack and setting course for the primary mission objective. They are to follow as soon as the enemy ships' nav systems are disabled."

Gears didn't wait for the order; he set course for Albanel and applied maximum thrust to the non-FTL engine. Nick watched with inner satisfaction as the image of the two damaged enemy vessels on his center screen shrank until they disappeared in the star-studded blackness of space. "Gears, how long until we reach Albanel?"

"We will be orbiting the planet in two point seven hours."

They may have been betrayed and set up for destruction, but as usual, Blaster Squad beat the odds. So far.

8

ANSS Lightning
Approaching planet Albanel
Gateway system
4154.3.26 Galactic

NICK SHIFTED IN his chair. He felt oddly uneasy, but much better overall after consuming two bottles of electrolyte fluid. "Clobe, what defenses are you reading?"

Mins Clobe responded immediately. "I'm reading a stealth ship or station orbiting the planet. It reads as very large, up to a kilometer in length, but the readings are somewhat defused given their stealth tech is more advanced than ours. Their patrol ships don't appear to have detected our approach so far. They are conducting passive sensor sweeps of the inner system, particularly in the area of Albanel and its three moons."

Nick lifted the cup of apple-flavored electrolyte fluid from the cup holder in his chair arm and took a sip. His lips and throat were still surprisingly dry.

The cool acidic fluid passed over his lips and he swallowed. *Why am I so on edge?*

"Gears," Nick began shifting his gaze to the pilot's seat next to him. Gears was focused on three screens in front of him recessed into the pilot's consol.

"Yes, sir?" he replied without taking the ocular implants he used for sight from the screens. He had lost his eyes many years ago when he was an engineer on an Alliance naval warship.

"How is it they have more advanced tech than we do? I thought *Thunder* and *Lightning* were the most advanced starships in the Alliance?"

Gears shrugged. "They are, as far as I know." He finally looked in Nick's direction. His lips were curled at the corners in a half-baked sardonic smile. "I'd like to get a look at those shields."

Nick chuckled. "Yeah, I know what you mean. As my old gramps used to say, 'There's everything new under the sun'." Gears snorted, then turned his attention back to his station screens.

"Stacks, any comm traffic?"

"Some. Nothing significant. Routine kind of stuff."

Suddenly Siren's frantic voice erupted over the comm.

"Nick! It's a trap. Head for the nearest moon. Now!"

"You heard her!" Nick said gripping the arms of his chair as Gears made a sudden course correction, straining the antigravity compensators to their maximum. A gray moon covered in craters with some signs of settlements across its surface came up rapidly on his center screen. "Get us in a close an orbit as possible. There's a chance it might mask our presence."

"*Thunder* signals they are joining us in orbit," said Stacks.

"Detecting launches from the moon's surface and six patrol ships have diverted from the area of the stealth ship orbiting Albanel," reported Clobe. His voice was calm and even. *He might work out after all*, thought Nick.

"Is our stealth shield fully operational?"

"Yes, Captain," said Gears. "While we were in transit, it took me thirty minutes to make the repairs." He grinned at Nick. "The book says it takes sixteen hours." Nick offered his friend a weak grin.

"Uh, excuse me, Captain," interrupted the SIN. "But the patrol vessels are converging on our coordinates."

"Stacks, signal Siren to get out of the system as fast as she's able." Nick ordered Clobe to bring up the positions of the incoming vessels on his screens. His brow wrinkled as he watched the enemy vessels' courses appear as green icons on the center screen. Yes, they did appear to be converging on them, and quickly. They could run but he recognized the pattern of the approaching vessels. It was a classic flanking maneuver. Any attempt to escape would be futile. They were moving to surround them.

"SIN, disengage the stealth shields and power down the engines. Bones, power down all weapons."

"What are you planning?" asked Gears.

"Surrender," said Nick, his voice devoid of any emotion.

"Sir?" said Stacks and Clobe in unison.

Bones grunted. "If the Cap'n says we surrender, then we surrender. You boys are going to learn the hard way what it means to be part of Blaster Squad."

"The enemy has us surrounded," reported the SIN.

"We're receiving a signal," said Stacks. "Huh, someone calling himself Stormcrow?"

Nick smiled to himself and his eyes narrowed as he glanced at Gears, who appeared surprised.

"I thought he was dead," Gears whispered.

Nick nodded. "Go ahead and put him through."

9

NICK STOOD ON the command deck of the space station or battlewagon—he still didn't know which—his wrists secured by force cuffs. Around him at the edge of the deck, standing at attention, were twenty guards dressed in black battle armor, their faces hidden by helmets with shaded faceplates. They held pulse rifles across their wide chests and had blasters secured in holsters around their waists. Behind them along a curved wall were workstations of some kind, each with a technician from a wide variety of planets throughout the Alliance. There were even a couple that looked like large crickets, of a race he had never seen before.

In the center of the room was a dais upon which sat an ornate chair Nick could only describe as a throne.

The empty throne was painted a gleaming black that reflected the subdued lighting of the command deck as if it were made from an obsidian crystal.

Nick smirked to himself. This all looked over the top but was in keeping with Stormcrow's usual modus operandi. Born under his real name, Percy Nicely, on Capella IV one hundred years ago to a working class family, he had adopted the brand Stormcrow when he started his mercenary company. He had been freelancing his services for the past seventy-five years. During his time in the game, Percy had amassed a massive fortune because, unlike Nick, he was willing to take on any contract. Whether it was legal or ethical or not made no difference. All Percy ever cared about was that his payday was substantial and paid in Alliance credits or its equivalent.

Of course, this was also his weakness, because Nick knew why Percy became who he was today. He was a bitter person who had lost everything he ever loved or cared about when his home world of Capella IV was wiped clean of all life by a to-this-day still unidentified enemy.

At the time, Percy and Nick had both been serving in the Alliance Navy together on the ANSS *Barack Obama*. That vessel was a light destroyer class ship, part of a flotilla headed for Capella IV.

The Capella government had transmitted an urgent request for help to navy headquarters, saying they were under attack. The nearest navy warships were in this flotilla, located within half a light year from the Capella system when they received their orders.

They arrived at the planet within five hours of receiving the orders but were too late to save the indigenous population and all animal, plant, and even insect life from being wiped off the planet. All that remained was a desert-like environment. Every lifeform had disappeared from the surface as if they never existed. Nine billion beings scrubbed from a world in a matter of hours.

There had been traces of a mysterious energy signature that led navy investigators to the edge of the system where the trail ended. On the planet they discovered a chemical residue of an unknown pathogen. Publicly, the flotilla commander concluded the enemy vessels had jumped to FTL before the flotilla arrived, but she didn't provide any details about what happened to the inhabitants of Capella IV.

A top secret report was later filed after a lengthy investigation, stating the Alliance was unable to determine how Capella IV had been wiped clean or who the perpetrators were.

Percy had never seen the report, but Nick managed to snag a clandestine copy of the report years later with the aid of his mentor, Asia Call, who had connections deep within the Alliance hierarchy. Percy resigned from the navy bitter and angry, telling Nick the Alliance didn't care about his world and vowed he'd make them pay for ignoring the extermination of his race.

The sound of a lift door opening behind Nick caused him to look over his right shoulder. He grinned to himself as he saw Percy enter the command deck dressed in a head-to-toe black outfit based on an Alliance Navy admiral's uniform, though heavily stylized with a nest of shiny medals covering his left breast and gleaming, calf-high boots.

He had even added a cape that waved, covering his wide shoulders and muscular frame like a shroud as he walked toward the throne in the center of the room. His square jaw was set and his ink-black hair touched his broad shoulders. His chiseled yellow features were marred by an angry glare as his dark eyes scanned the room, passing over Nick as if he were transparent, moving with a sense of purpose across the deck. His polished thigh high boots thumped loudly against the plasti-steel plates with each long-legged stride.

Nick followed the mercenary leader's progress until he eventually sat on the throne. At his right, standing at attention, was a human male aide dressed in a similar albeit toned-down version of his uniform. Percy's scowling features studied a three dimensional image that was being projected from the arm of the chair. The depiction of the rotating blue-and-green world looked to Nick like a representation of the planet they were orbiting—if they hadn't left orbit after his capture—though it was speckled with colored dots, too many to easily count. He concluded the dots must represent something that was bothering Percy given his expression, but Nick could only guess what was on the mercenary leader's mind.

A tall, slender woman approached Percy. She was dressed in a dark blue uniform tunic and slate gray pants. Her angular smoke-gray face and brilliant blue eyes betrayed her origins as one of the lower caste Estuian peoples. Her race had been forced into slavery by the upper castes for generations. Her deep purple hair brushed her shoulders with each step until she stood in front of the throne at attention, waiting for her commander's attention in silence. She did not so much as glance in Nick's direction.

Nick studied her bearing and her eyes and decided this was no slave.

She exuded the confidence of a senior officer.

"Yes, centurion," Percy said finally, his deep voice echoing across the command deck. His eyes remained fixated on the image of the rotating Albanel.

"Tribune, we have lost contact with the second enemy starship."

Percy's gaze shifted to look at the woman. With an arched eyebrow, he regarded her with intensity in his eyes that Nick could feel from where he stood. Before he spoke, Percy's brow wrinkled. "Failure is *not* acceptable."

The woman looked away, her eyes focused on the deck, her head bowed slightly forward. Her cheeks had flushed darker and Nick noticed her hands trembling. "Yes, sir. They disappeared from the sensors after we captured the other vessel." She cleared her throat, then added, "We did capture their commander. Sir."

Percy's facial expression eased and his shoulders relaxed slightly. He slowly nodded his head. "Yes, I see you have. But you had better locate that other ship soon or there will be serious consequences." The centurion's features drained of color. "Dismissed," Percy said curtly.

The centurion raised her right arm across her chest parallel to the deck, then tapped her closed fist against the left side of her chest. She spun round and walked away, her back to Percy, across the command deck to disappear behind lift doors.

Percy snorted loudly followed by a grim chuckle. "Why is it always like that between us, Nicky?" He stood and his cape flowed to his side to reveal his muscular form. Nick saw the short sword in a scabbard hanging on his left hip and a blaster in a holster on his right. He hadn't noticed Percy was carrying weapons until now. Not that it worried him. Percy and he went way back, so the mercenary leader wasn't about to kill him out of hand.

Then again, the last time they had seen each other was at that bar on Putin Station near the Mutara sector. His somewhat foggy memory suggested their parting company hadn't ended that well. He seemed to recall something about their respective mothers and missing teeth. *Wasn't there a best beer guzzler contest? He wouldn't kill me over a disagreement about ales versus pilsners?* Or would he?

Nick chuckled derisively. "Finally noticed me eh, Percy?"

Percy grunted and his haggard features darkened. "My name is Stormcrow and you know it, Nick."

Nick shrugged. "I'm the one in restraints. Call yourself anything you wish but I'll always think of you as good old Percy Nicely, junior weapons officer assigned to the ANSS *Barack Obama*."

One corner of Percy's mouth curled slightly and he arched one eyebrow. He barked a derisive laugh. "Now you're just trying to provoke me." He stood and stepped off the dais. He strolled slowly over to stand in front of Nick as his right hand swept aside the cape revealing he had placed a hand on the butt of the blaster pistol. "I could just have you executed Nicky, but you and I go back a long way." His eyes suddenly darkened and his gaze shifted away to his left for a second or two, then back to lock on Nick. "I'm hoping you'll help me before I have to do something I really don't want to do."

Nick hadn't followed his old friend's gaze; instead, he kept his eyes locked on his body language. Being able to determine a person's actions if they were speaking truthfully was an acquired skill, something he had worked hard at since he was a naval cadet decades ago. He had become quite adept at reading the most logical outcome of situations. Most importantly, he had never shared that he had this skill with anyone.

Of course, Gears had known him for so long he certainly knew about it—though they had never spoken about each other's special skills—but the pilot wasn't about to share this information with anyone.

But the former junior naval officer seated on his pretentious throne certainly had no idea about Nick's abilities. He probably wanted Nick's help based on their shared history and the reputation Blaster Squad had garnered over the years.

Until he knew more about what Percy was up to, he wasn't going to agree to anything. Even when he had all the information, he might not agree. If this was the case, Percy's body language suggested he was deadly serious, which meant he might just have Nick and his crew executed if they refused. Nick would need a strategy to deal with this possible outcome. But this would take time and planning with the cooperation of his crew. Time he might not have.

"Okay, Stormcrow, why don't you tell me more about what's been going on here?" He let his gaze drift around the room until once again landing on the ruddy complexion of the would-be warlord or whatever he considered himself. The use of titles like centurion reminded Nick of something he'd heard before but he couldn't quite place it.

He would make a point of asking the SIN about it when he had the opportunity. "It seems you have a considerable amount of force at your beck and call."

Stormcrow winced slightly before replying. "Yes, we do have considerable firepower, but they seem to have a knack for hiding…" his words trailed off.

Nick suppressed a laugh. "Okay, I get it. First, remove these restraints so we can talk." Stormcrow nodded to one his guards, who came over and deactivated the force cuffs. Nick rubbed his wrists where the energy bands had contacted his skin. "And second, who are *they*?"

Stormcrow walked across the deck, his footsteps echoing on the deck plates. On one wall was a large screen that was dark at the moment. "Screen on," Stormcrow said.

The screen came on, displaying a map of the planet they were orbiting. At least a section of the planet Nick immediately recognized as the planet's largest plasma ore mining operation. This was the crown jewel of the economics of the Alliance and was needed to power the fleet to maintain order in the galaxy. Whoever hired Stormcrow and his mercenaries wanted to wrest control of these resources from the Alliance, hoping this would allow them to conquer the galaxy.

While there were other Alliance worlds with plasma ore, none had the quantities available on Albanel.

Nick's larger problem was he had to stop Perc... correction, Stormcrow from taking over the planet. To accomplish this he might have to help the mercenary leader in order to gain his trust. It was the one sure way—and the best way he could think of right now— to discovering the true identity of the Master.

Stormcrow's cheeks flushed bright yellow and he averted his eyes. Nick realized his old friend was embarrassed. Finally the mercenary leader cleared his throat. "We were beating back the locals when someone landed from off-planet and provided logistical support. Coupled with the local rebels, they managed to not only stop the progression of my forces but also push them back. We've not been able to break them for the past two months."

Nick arched an eyebrow and regarded Stormcrow with his arms crossed over his chest. "How can that be? You have more firepower at your disposal than most Alliance Navy battle groups."

"They have a cunning leader now...a woman named Sonar, or something like that, who is highly skilled at guerilla tactics."

Stormcrow snorted his frustration and a look of anger mingled with frustration passed over his rugged features. "I haven't used guerilla tactics in decades. I lead an army that usually crushes my opponents into submission." He moved to his throne and sat down, his cape draping around him like a shroud once again.

Nick thought for several seconds. Of course Percy had to be talking about Sonara, Siren's sister. Suddenly he erupted in a sharp bark of laughter, startling Stormcrow out of his defeated mood. "Well then, Stormy, old boy, I guess we need a banana peel for this Sonar to slip on, don't we. I think my team and I can provide the fruit if you provide the transportation."

Stormcrow glared at him. "The name's *Stormcrow,* not *Stormy.* " His angry expression eased. "I guess we can get you to the surface without being detected."

Nick chuckled. "Great. This is gonna be a slice of cake with pie on top."

A crooked, not-amused-in-the-least smile passed over Stormcrow's features as he shook his head in disgust.

10

NICK READ THE readouts in the battle helmet's
faceplate and saw they had materialized five
kilometers from the mining facility. It was night,
so the suit had automatically adjusted to night
operations, giving the local ripped-up rock and dirt a
soft green glow. Gears stood next to him, his blaster
rifle at the ready, his eyes flitting across the devastated
landscape looking for threats.

According to the SIN, the planet had been covered
with lush green forests in the not too distant past,
but the recent battles had destroyed the foliage and
much of the greenery, and the indigenous animal life
had been scoured off this world. Carpet bombing and
heavy weapons tended to play hell on the local flora
and fauna.

Blaster Squad #6 Galaxy of Evil

According to Percy, or Stormcrow as he now called himself, the only lifeforms surviving the Armageddon inflicted by Stormcrow's fleet was of the humanoid variety. Very curious, actually. How had Sonara's rebels managed to survive the dead landscape he was looking at?

"Gears, you getting any lifeform readings?" Nick asked.

It had taken some doing but Nick convinced Stormcrow he and Gears alone could make contact with this Sonar rebel leader and find out what they wanted in trade for leaving the world to Stormcrow and his real boss, the Master. Not that Stormcrow admitted the Master had hired him, but Nick certainly wanted to believe it. Especially when Stormcrow shared why he wanted to defeat Sonar and the rebels soon.

Stormcrow had been provided a weapon that could unleash a burst of deadly energy that would cause the planet to implode, eliminating the valuable plasma ore but also every lifeform on the planet. His orders were to destroy the planet so the Alliance couldn't use the plasma to fuel their fleet to oppose the Master's forces if they couldn't take control of the ore.

Stormcrow's description of the energy in this weapon reminded him of the report he'd read years ago about the energy source stolen some thirteen years ago from the Alliance experimental weapons laboratory at Area 51 in the Nevada desert on Earth. The energy had never been used as far as they knew, and the perpetrator had never been apprehended. Whoever stole this deadly energy had been on the Alliance's most wanted list in the years since the theft, yet not one single clue had ever been found nor had there been any leads for investigators to follow. Until now.

And Nick and Blaster Squad were smack in the middle of something far larger and far more important than the mission they had signed on for. It was like being the protein in a crap sandwich. *Actually, no it isn't.*

Nick looked at the sensor feed on his helmet screen and saw the mining installation was five kilometers away. Though the terrain was rough, they could hike to the location in a few hours. "Gears, let's head out. We have a long hike ahead of us."

Gears grunted. "No, not really."

"We're five kilometers from the objectiv—"

Gears snorted derisively, cutting him off. "That *isn't* the issue, Captain."

Nick felt a growing knot of anger forming in the pit of his stomach. "Then what is?" he said between gritted teeth.

"The fact is we're surrounded so we won't have to hike anywhere."

11

Somewhere on the surface of Albanel
Gateway system
4154.3.27 Galactic

THESE DAMNED FORCE *cuffs really itch.* Nick looked to his left, where two burly rebels stood eyeing him as if he were fish bait. They were wearing identical head-to-toe burnished black blast armor. Neither were human, but both looked as mean as the nastiest human who had ever lived. They were two different species neither he recognized. One was twirling a long, thick-bladed knife that gleamed in the low light coming from the strip lamps affixed to the cave's ceiling. The other guard was busily polishing the body of a large blaster rifle. The air was warm and smelled vaguely of machine oil mingled with a nose burning burnt ozone smell. A slight breeze to moderate the acrid stench came from the opening to the corridor they'd brought him in through after he was captured.

Nick cleared his throat and squished his face as if he'd sucked on a sour fruit.

The guard with the knife had stopped the twirling and now regarded him with one eyebrow arched. Its gray eyes narrowed and its pasty white features were marred by a glare. "What ya doin', uman?" The voice sounded female but the alien's appearance suggested male.

"Nothing," Nick said. "But this cave smells *really* bad." He shifted his gaze between the two guards. "Or maybe it's you two that reek?"

The guard cleaning the blaster set the butt of the rifle on the cave floor and shifted its right hand on the butt of the blaster pistol in the holster. "You insult us, uman?"

Nick snorted. "I'm merely complaining about the odor in here. Surely you could have brought me into a better smelling cave than this dump."

The two guards exchanged a look that he was unable to discern what it might mean. The guard with the knife pressed a button on the breastplate of its blast armor. "Rels to command."

"Go head," came the immediate reply.

"The prisoner wants the commander."

Did I say that? Nick grinned and nodded. He would play along, hoping to eventually find Sonara and some answers.

These aliens were a strange lot, but since he'd never met this race before, their actions could actually be perfectly normal.

"Hey, Nick, how're you doing?"

Nick froze, then slowly turned to look at the entrance to discover Sonara Albright standing with her fists on her hips. She was dressed in head-to-toe gleaming black armor identical to the guards, her black hair pulled back away from her narrow pale face, a sardonic grin on her lips. Her eyes sparked as she surveyed him in his restraints where he was seated on a rocky shelf at the opposite end of the cave.

She dropped her arms to her sides, then entered the cave striding toward him, her eyes locked on his. Her right hand rested on the butt of the blaster in the holster hanging off her right hip. A bandolier worn sash style over her right shoulder containing blaster rifle charge cartridges rattled as she walked. It was then he noticed her face was smudged with soot and she had a slight limp favoring her left leg. Sonara had been in a fight very recently.

She stopped just far enough away that, if he tried to attack her, the guards would have the drop on him before he laid a finger on her.

She offered him a sardonic lopsided smile and crossed her long arms over her chest.

"Got nothing to say, Nick Justice, leader of Blaster Squad?"

Nick grunted his reply, then shrugged while maintaining a bland expression on his face.

Sonara laughed grimly and her expression darkened as her amusement gave way to a serious expression and her eyes narrowed. "We don't have time for games, Nick. Your pal Stormcrow is going to unleash his weapon on us and wipe out all life on this world. According to reports I've read, the planet will be uninhabitable for a couple of centuries."

Nick nodded grimly. "Yes, I know. I've read the same reports."

Sonara arched an eyebrow looking at him, her eyes quizzical. "So you're not working with Stormcrow?"

"No." Nick rolled his eyes. "Of course not. My mission is to secure access to the plasma ore for the Alliance. And to stop the Master's forces from gaining control of the ore."

Sonara snorted derisively. "Well, it seems you've pretty much failed on both counts so far."

Nick nodded.

"I was hired by private interests to discover the identity of the Master. I plan to capture Stormcrow alive and get the information I need to find the Master."

Nick shifted his gaze to lock eyes with Siren's sister. "Then why are you helping the rebels defeat Stormcrow's forces?"

She looked away and shrugged. "I can't ignore these people's suffering. I have to do something."

It dawned on Nick that Sonara might not be all bad after all. She had interfered in several of his operations these past few years, leaving havoc in her wake. But something inside him told him she had changed. She had betrayed them more than once in the past. On the plus side, she had helped them successfully complete several important missions. Somehow he would justify this latest alliance with her. For now.

Or someone was paying her a pile of credits to change. Either way, she might be the ally he needed to defeat Stormcrow and complete his mission objectives.

"You sister escaped when my ship was captured," he said in a low voice, the deep timber of his tone echoing off the cave walls.

She looked at him with a slow grin spreading across her narrow features. He knew then this mission was going to be complicated but the odds of success had just risen. There was still a lot of work to be done to defeat the massive firepower aimed directly at them. And if they failed, Blaster Squad would be dead—that much was certain.

12

NICK'S BREATH CAME faster as they made the run across the compound to the side of the temporary machine shop set up by Stormcrow's engineer techs. The stealth suit Sonara provided made him warmer than normal. It wasn't the latest in stealth tech, but if it made him invisible to the enemy, he would be happy to suffer a little physical discomfort.

Sonara had been able to contact her sister via a scrambled, narrow beam comm system she had smuggled onto the planet's surface earlier when she and her team of mercenaries materialized on their present coordinates.

The sight of the heavily armed Alliance Navy shock troopers in her party made him uneasy. He'd been told they were all retired from the navy and were now working with her on clandestine missions to penetrate the Master's forces wherever they were discovered.

At first it made sense that the new Alliance chair would hire more than one mercenary team, but then he witnessed them methodically vaporize a field hospital for Stormcrow's soldiers they landed near when they transported to this area of the planet. He wondered then if he'd made a mistake agreeing to team up with Sonara.

Nick pulled his blaster pistol from the holster on his hip and crept along with his back to the wall of the shop. The shop doors were open and he hadn't seen any guards when he surveyed the site prior to making his way down the cliffs to the canyon floor. He suspected this was considered a quiet area so security would be lacking. Or so he hoped.

Following close behind him was Sonara and six of her mercenaries, also wearing stealth suits. Their footsteps over the uneven ground were muffled by the stealth boots; he only wished his suit had an olfactory stealth feature. Nick had been sweating profusely since they landed two hours ago and began the hike cross-country to the site of this installation. The sour scent of his sweat filled his nose and his mouth and it wasn't pleasant. He would enjoy the long shower after the mission more than usual.

The sound of a single click over the comm told him to stop moving.

He glanced at Sonara and saw she was using hand signals to indicate there were security cameras near the entrance. And no doubt there were ground sensors installed as well. They had to be careful or they'd lose the element of surprise. Sonara had out her hand scanner and was intent now on the small screen of the device.

She looked from the screen to Nick and he saw she had a wide grin on her lips. He nodded and his heart rate increased. This meant there was a fully functioning air tank inside the facility.

The plan was coming together nicely.

They would steal the air tank, booby-trap it with explosives, then fly it into the main supply base used by Stormcrow's assault troops. Hilo Tiks, Siren's ship's engineer, had transported to the surface from the *Thunder,* now in synchronous orbit with their position, to help them to make the tank operational and rig it to explode at the right time.

Tiks would also set up a comm link to fly the tank by remote control to the target so none of them would have to sacrifice themselves in delivering a blow to the enemy.

Nick was especially worried about his crew. Gears, Bones, Clobe, and Stacks were still being held aboard Stormcrow's command ship.

This part of the plan, concocted by the two sisters, Sonara and Siren, was to assault Stormcrow's command ship with a rapid strike by the *Thunder,* hoping to catch them while they were distracted by the attack on the surface. If she managed to take out the shields of Stormcrow's vessel, Siren, who would be on the surface, would simultaneously use the materializer to board the *Dark Storm* and free his crew. It had to be perfectly timed and executed and the enemy had to cooperate by being actually distracted, which depended on how well they were trained.

Siren would then leave orbit at a high rate of speed and hide on one of the many moons in the system until she could come back and rescue Nick, Sonara, and her shock troop mercenaries.

Timing and execution were the keys to success and this worried Nick because, in his experience, any operation this dependent on perfect execution was too often knocked off the rails by unanticipated events. He didn't know exactly where the term *knocked off the rails* originated other than it meant their plans would fall apart if anything went wrong. Nick swallowed hard at the thought of Stormcrow taking his revenge for the attack on him and his crew.

The mercenary leader's reputation for torture to make his victims suffer terrible agony until they begged for death was well known in mercenary circles. Nick hoped they'd be able to complete the mission unscathed, but the odds had been stacked against since the beginning.

Tiks reached into a hidden compartment in the blast armor on his chest and pulled out a device unlike anything Nick had ever seen. It looked like a miniature old-fashioned personal transmitter with a touch pad on the front and two depressions. In the low light it was hard to see any details other than that because it was dull black in color.

Tiks used his gloved thumb to press one of the depressions. Immediately Nick held his breath when he heard one of the guards near the entrance to the facility shout something to his comrades. He couldn't make out what exactly the guard said but the other guard moved quickly to a flanking position near the entrance; soon they were joined by two more heavily armed guards who moved to opposite sides of the entrance, their rifles held at the ready as they scanned the tree line.

Tiks nodded to Sonora, who signaled they were to split into two teams and move into position through the thick stands of leafy trees to the right and left of the entrance. Once they were in position, the plan called for the troopers and Tiks to lay down suppressing fire with their blaster rifles while Sonara and Nick lobbed concussion grenades near the guards to disable them.

Tiks' device was supposed to render the surveillance cameras and the ground sensors inoperable. As Nick began to move as quickly and quietly as possible into the forest, he hoped Tiks was as good as Gears at this tech stuff or this operation would come to an end before it began.

The ground underfoot was spongy with rotting vegetation so it muffled their footsteps. They carefully made their way through the wide leaves of the plants, trying not to make too much noise. Some of the thick, dark green tree trunks covered in large leaves the size of serving platters extended forty meters or more over their heads. Their armor was non-reflective, so even the exterior lights on the installation wouldn't give away their position once they turned off the stealth feature, which they would do once the signal was given.

The hope was if the guards saw attackers suddenly appear, they would think there were more attackers lurking the perimeter of the facility waiting to join the fight.

Some might even give up, though knowing how much fear Stormcrow had instilled in his troopers if they failed, this was highly unlikely.

Finally they came to the designated position and Nick sucked in a breath. He tapped his comm button twice to indicate they had arrived and he heard a similar reply immediately. Sonara and her team were ready. Letting his breath out slowly, he holstered his blaster pistol, then took a grenade off the specially designed holder on his weapons belt.

He waited, wondering if something had gone wrong. It was taking too long for the go signal. He stiffened when a double click came over the comm in his helmet. Counting to ten as they'd arranged, he nodded to the three mercenaries with him and Tiks when he'd counted to eight. They held their blaster rifles at the ready, waiting for his hand signal to turn off the stealth shield and begin firing at the four guards that were visible. The guards would be dead after the first blaster shots if the grenade didn't kill them.

During planning, what worried them most of all were the numbers of additional guards inside the facility who had no doubt been alerted to the loss of the sensors and the cameras.

The readings from orbit were unclear about the number of troops at the facility, and readings on the ground were likewise inconclusive.

He hoped the Intel had been correct about there really being a working air tank inside. If there wasn't a functioning air tank, then once again the mission would be over before it started. Nick really hated missions with intelligence made of Swiss cheese.

Early in the planning, he had briefly considered abandoning the plan altogether but he had to free his crew from Stormcrow regardless of the risks, so he decided to go ahead regardless of the risks hoping it worked out for the best. And with his fingers and toes crossed for good luck. He didn't exactly know how a physical gesture would help but his grandfather told him stories about a time when people believed in luck, so anything that might give them the edge he was willing to do.

At the count of ten, he heaved the grenade in the direction of the guards. Form the corner of one eye he spotted the second grenade on its way to the target.

Tiks and the mercenaries began to fire as they became visible, moving to their left, then their right to add to the illusion there were more blasters firing than there were.

The tactic wouldn't work for more than a few seconds but any additional time it added to the confusion of combat was vital to their success.

The four guards each got off a few shots before the grenades exploded and they were thrown off their feet by the concussion wave. They were lying still, their limbs askew, their weapons thrown out of easy reach. If they managed to get to their blasters, his team and Sonara's would shoot them before they were able to return fire.

The more pressing problem was the eight heavily armed and heavily armored shock troopers who appeared from the entrance of the repair facility. The troopers began firing as soon as they rushed into view.

A surge of super-heated plasma flowed past Nick as one of the troopers fired in his direction. He realized the trooper wasn't aiming at him when the mercenary to his left grunted and began to glow, then shimmer before it dissolved into nothingness as its muscular frame disappeared in the plasma energy.

"Stealth. Break L. Eight," he whispered in a low, harsh tone over his comm while activating his stealth armor. He shifted left to the eight o'clock position as planned and hurried to flank the enemy troopers who continued to fire where he had been only milliseconds before. He grinned to himself.

The tactic had worked.

Nick removed a second grenade off his belt and stopped forty meters from the targets. He activated the grenade's fuse, then threw it to a spot in the middle of the enemy troopers. He then shifted another few degrees, this time to his right, and began quickly moving away, his boot steps sighing in the soft fertile ground. His heart raced from the adrenaline coursing through his blood stream. The thrill of battle always made him feel more alive than anything else ever had.

The grenade exploded, emitting a dull thud accompanied by a brilliant flash, sending a cloud of smoke riddled with chunks of dirt into the air obscuring his view of the enemy.

"Eyes on?" he said.

"Not down. Repeat. Not down," came the reply from a mercenary on Sonara's team whose name he didn't recall.

Nick's mind raced. This meant the enemy was wearing personal shields. How had Stormcrow acquired personal shields? The tech was beyond top secret. At least that's what Gears said when they used the tech during a previous mission. It was covert ops stuff, not general issue; even Alliance naval personnel serving as crew on Alliance warships were not issued personal shields.

Nick's heart seemed to freeze as the realization struck him that someone on the Alliance board had provided the devices to Stormcrow. This confirmed his old frienemey was indeed employed by the Master.

"Set weapons to stun." There were no acknowledgements as he changed his blaster's setting, so he hoped the mercenaries had changed their blaster's settings too. If they hadn't, then the charge he was about to order would end badly.

"Frontal," he said under his breath. Turning toward the entrance, he started a headlong run at the knot of troopers firing into the tree line. He dropped two immediately before two more shifted their fire in his direction. Nick shifted to his left and stopped firing. The plasma fire coming from the enemy troopers vaporized a couple of trees where he had just been. He continued to race toward the troopers until he was within fifty meters of their position. He stopped, his breathing measured. He aimed his blaster at the nearest three and fired; they dropped heavily to the ground. He then quickly moved to his right, careful not to disturb tree branches.

The enemy troopers fired at where he had just been. There were only two enemy troopers left standing.

As he watched, the remaining two troopers dropped to the ground unconscious as they were engulfed in multiple stun beams coming from several directions.

"All clear," he heard Sonara say over the comm.

Tapping his stealth button on his chest plate, Nick became visible, as did Sonara and five other mercenaries. Tiks appeared last to the left side of the entrance to the repair facility. "Hold your position, Tiks, until we complete a sweep inside." Tiks looked in Nick's direction and nodded he understood. They would need the tech's expertise so Nick wasn't taking any chances.

Nick nodded to two of the mercenaries standing beside Sonara, who shot annoyed glances at each other before entering the facility. Within a few seconds they signaled all clear over the comm.

Sonara came up beside Nick, her rifle now slung around her torso by the strap. She slapped his shoulder and he glanced at her. Her blast visor was up and he could see her wide grin. "Not bad, eh?" she said cheerfully.

Nick's gut twisted. "How many did we lose?"

She shrugged and her grin faded, her brow wrinkling slightly. "What does it matter? We won the position. That's all that truly matters.

"I love it when a plan comes together."

Nick grunted and his gaze traveled over the fallen troopers and mercenaries who hadn't been vaporized, strewn haphazardly across the ground in front of the repair facility as if they were broken children's toys. Some were dead, some were stunned into unconsciousness. The stunned enemy troopers would revive long after they were gone. "I wear death every day," he said, unable to keep the bitterness from his voice.

"I found the perfect air tank we need," Tiks said over the comm, his voice tinged with excitement.

"Understood," replied Nick, his stomach muscles tightening. Now they needed the pilot for the air tank, who would undertake the next phase of the mission. The most dangerous phase.

13

Stormcrow's forward assault base
Albanel
Gateway system
4154.3.29 Galactic

SIREN PUNCHED THE comm button on the flight
console in front of her. The thick, lush forest visible
on the external monitor spread across the horizon in
the distance as she flew the speeding air tank low over
the tall trees and giant fronds being tossed about by
the displacement of the speeding air tank's wake. The
growl of the thrusters filled the cramped cabin.

The glove covering the fingers of her right
hand was thick since they were designed for a large
trooper. Pressing the control surfaces of the console
was cumbersome. Air tanks didn't have a System
Information Network, meaning everything had to be
done manually by the pilot. *So old-fashioned*, she
mused.

She had donned one of the dead guard's uniforms
hoping to disguise herself to get past the guards.

The uniform was the smallest she could find but it was still ill fitting over her lean frame and was like wearing a tent.

"Base to unidentified tank. You have five seconds to respond." The voice was high-pitched, probably a Lucsian. When they spoke galactic standard, for some unknown reason their voices became oddly high-pitched compared to when they spoke their own language.

"This is Trooper One-seven-six-five-alpha," she said without hesitation, reciting the trooper's number from where she found it in the display graphics inside the visor. She added an edge of impatience into her tone. "My engines are over-heating. I require immediate clearance before I'm vaporized by a ball of fiery destruction."

"We have scanned your ship, verified its code, and your identity number is confirmed. Proceed to landing field seventeen. Confirm."

For a brief second Siren considered a snide reply but instead acknowledged the instructions in her best bureaucratic-boredom voice. Grinning to herself because what she really wanted to do was kick some Lucsian butt right now, but her phase of the mission took priority over her personal whims.

She sighted the landing field she'd been directed to and confirmed the protective screens had been dropped. So far the plan was working.

There were six support vehicles that would be her welcoming committee and no signs of armed troopers who might know the trooper who usually wore this uniform. She didn't want an armed confrontation this early in her mission.

When the tank was hovering over the landing field, she activated the landing skids and set the craft on the ground. The engine whine immediately tapered off as the engines shut down upon contact with the ground. Now for the real test of her disguise.

The hatch door at the rear of the flight compartment swung up revealing two techs who entered the crowded space before she could exit. Thankfully they were slightly built humans who were focused on the tank's systems more than her.

Tiks had rigged the tank's systems to report the damage to the engines and weapons as Siren had stated over the comm.

One of the techs, a woman, wore a deep frown and was shaking her head in disgust. "Someone has abused the systems," she muttered, her hazel eyes focused on the readout screen on a handheld scanner in her left hand.

The man next to her snorted derisively. "Yeah, Beeks, they really kicked the crap out of this poor tank."

"Do you need me for anything?" Siren asked, edging her way closer to the open hatch.

Neither tech took their eyes off their scanners as the woman responded. "No. We'll take it from here, trooper."

Seeing her chance to escape, Siren marched out the hatch into the open landing field, but not before hearing the Beeks woman complain to her partner about troopers' lack of respect for the tools of their trade. Siren smirked.

The field was scarred black by the many takeoffs and landings of the various craft of war used by Stormcrow's forces. Before leaving the *Thunder,* she'd had the AI surreptitiously scan the records of Stormcrow's AI. It had been surprisingly easy for her AI to penetrate Stormcrow's records.

According to the AI, Stormcrow had landed some quarter of a million troops on the planet in attempt to quash any opposition by the locals to his occupation. So far over sixty thousand of his troops had been killed, wounded, or were missing, and he had yet to secure a beachhead on the planet.

During this process some five thousand drop ships, fifteen thousand air tanks, hundreds of suborbital fighters, and other equipment had been badly damaged or destroyed outright. Further, the locals weren't about to surrender the plasma ore without a fight, no matter how many had to die.

According to the AI, almost a million of the planet's inhabitants had died already, and if Stormcrow unleashed the energy weapon, the remaining billion plus would be snuffed out like a burned-out light bulb. She had no idea what a light bulb was but Nick had used the expression several times during their association to refer to genocide. And this would be genocide if the weapon were deployed. This is where her mission came in. She was to prevent the destruction of the inhabitants of this world and stop Stormcrow from robbing the plasma ore for the Master.

If they lost the plasma, then the Alliance would very likely fall and the galaxy would be ruled by evil. It would become a galaxy of evil. Siren had to stop herself from snorting at the thought of ever having to say those words out loud. Galaxy of evil was such a corny name but it was the origin of Percy Nicely's assumed persona, Stormcrow.

In the late thirty-second century, a popular virtual reality game called Galaxy of Evil involved a despot warlord named Stormcrow. Percy—who apparently was a rabid fan of ancient VR games—adopted the name as his persona in the new empire envisioned by the Master.

It all sounded stupid to Siren. *It is what it is*, she mused when the SIN provided the background information about the mercenary leader.

Pushing aside her amused indifference, she strode across the field to enter the building erected to house a comm and a materializer for moving crews and equipment to and from the planet and Stormcrow's command ship *Dark Storm* in orbit.

Now all she had to do was use the materializer to board the *Dark Storm*, plant a bomb to disable the vessel's defensive screens, free Gears, Clobe, Stacks, and Bones from the enemy brig, and get them aboard the *Lightning* currently in the ship's vessel bay. She would then help them escape—without being destroyed as soon as they exited the vessel—by disabling the *Dark Storm's* weapons systems.

After both *Lightning* and *Thunder* were clear, they would fire everything they had at the most vulnerable sections of the *Dark Storm*, which wouldn't be shielded.

It would be destroyed, ending the threat to Albanel and the Alliance, and hopefully taking out Stormcrow. But Siren wasn't so sure the mercenary leader wouldn't escape. He had been a survivor for a long time. He wasn't a priority anyway so Siren didn't care much. She just called his demise "bonus carnage" or something like that. She was never sure if she was using Nick's silly sayings correctly. Hopefully they'd transport her aboard one of the two Blaster Squad ships before *Dark Storm* became a miniature star.

Approaching the officer commanding the materializer operators, she said, "Sir, I seek permission to be transported to the sick bay aboard Dark Storm."

The officer, a grim-faced Estuian female, eyed her up and down, one eyebrow arched. "What's your issue?"

Siren had prepared for this moment. She pulled off a section of armor on her left leg revealing a bloody, oozing gash about half a meter in length. "I was wounded during a firefight with the local scum."

The officer grimaced and nodded. "Step on the platform."

"But, sir—" protested one of the two operators.

"Keep your mouths shut," snapped the officer. "I know she doesn't have any orders but she's one of our heroic troopers." Scowling at the operator who'd spoken, she added, "This trooper has no doubt done more to win this planet in one day than you two have done in your four months on this hunk of rock. She's earned the right to transport wherever and whenever she likes."

The two operators averted their eyes, focusing on the control console of the materializer. Their faces flushed a deep red.

"Thank you, sir," said Siren, stepping into the platform, and she almost meant it. These so-called mercenaries gave her profession a bad name. They were killers and thugs no better than the Scolsi rebels who killed her brother and her other sister twenty years ago during the Helos rebellion on Sigma III.

The officer remained stone-faced but did offer a slight nod of her head before Siren felt the familiar tingle of the materializer beam freezing her where she stood. The room faded, quickly replaced with a materializer chamber aboard what was obviously a spacecraft—but was it the right spacecraft?

Her answer came sooner than she thought it would.

Beside the control console stood a tall human male dressed head-to-toe in gleaming black armor. He wore a lopsided grin on his stubble-covered, narrow features and his dark eyes seemed to look right through her. Of course his most notable feature was the large blaster pistol gripped in his right hand aimed directly at her.

"Welcome to the *Dark Storm*, Sirenna Albright," he said in a deep baritone voice.

14

GSS Dark Storm
Orbiting Albanel
Gateway system
4154.3.29 Galactic

SIREN CONSIDERED DRAWING her blaster, then
stopped and sucked in a deep breath, then parted her
lips slightly to release the air slowly from her lungs.
Steady. An alternate strategy occurred to her.

"What is the meaning of this? I came here to
use the sick bay. I'm wounded." She slipped off
her helmet, then set it on the console. "And who is
Sirenna All…"

The tall, muscular man smiled grimly and his eyes
narrowed. But was that a slight flash of doubt in his
eyes? "You are Sirenna Albright and you're a member
of Blaster Squad."

Siren snorted derisively and shook her head. "My
name is Trooper One-seven-six-five-alpha. My unit
was assigned to protect a repair facility for damaged
air tanks. We were attacked by rebels." Her eyes
hardened.

"We killed them but suffered severe losses in the fight." She slipped off the gloves and set them next to the helmet. "Which way to the sick bay?"

The man lowered his weapon until finally holstering it. A frown wrinkled his brow. "I was told you were her." Siren saw the confusion on his face.

"Who exactly told you I was this Sirenna person?" She arched one eyebrow to emphasize how his questions annoyed her.

"Intelligence…" he said, his eyes growing wider as he realized she had her blaster out of her holster aimed at him.

"My code name is Siren, actually." She depressed the firing stud and a beam of super-heated energy ripped a hole in his chest armor right where his heart was located.

He emitted a soft gurgling sound as blood trickled from both sides of his mouth until he sagged to the deck, then fell forward facedown, landing with a loud smack. She moved to stand over him and kicked him in his side with no response. He was dead, all right. Dragging the body across the deck she did her best to conceal the corpse behind a bulkhead. It wouldn't take long to be discovered but hopefully she'd have completed her mission by then.

Intelligence? It struck her maybe he was talking about a spy. Normal procedure dictated enemy forces were to be infiltrated by spies, so it wouldn't surprise her if the locals had been compromised. But he knew her name. How? Had Blaster Squad been infiltrated? Were the new crewmembers she'd recruited to fly *Thunder* working for the Master and his minions?

After holstering her pistol, Siren moved to the comm unit recessed into the wall behind the operator's console.

Maybe I should have let him live long enough to tell me who told him my name. Her eyes shifted momentarily to the cooling corpse on the deck. *No. I did the right thing.*

She pressed the voice interface button on the comm panel. "SIN, this is Trooper One-seven-six-five-alpha requesting location of prisoners Musty Hobbs and Rocky Bones." She hoped Stacks and Clobe were at the same location, or at least nearby. She didn't want to overplay her hand by using all their names.

"Detention area three, deck seven," replied the AI without hesitation.

Pulling the portable comm unit off her weapons belt, she said, "Transmit the fastest route to that location to my comm unit."

The unit beeped in milliseconds as it received the requested information. It was amazing how loud the beep sounded in the quiet materializer room.

Siren stepped back and studied the route provided on the holo projection now hovering in the air coming from her comm unit and felt her blood grow cold. The projection was of the entire vessel and a brilliant green line showed the quickest route to deck seven, where her friends were being held and no doubt tortured.

She was going to have to go through some heavily populated areas of the ship to get there. And no doubt there would be heavily armed guards much more ready than this pompous jerk to shoot first and ask questions afterward. Why this guy didn't even have an armed escort with him really made her wonder. But then, overconfident fools are easily separated from their lives by their own stupidity.

On the other hand this could all be an elaborate trap, though at this point that seemed unlikely.

She headed for the exit to the corridors beyond. According to the map, the lift was to the left not more than twenty meters. Her right hand rested on the butt of her blaster in her holster just in case the rest of a reception committee was behind the doors and she had to shoot it out.

The doors parted and slid aside to reveal an empty corridor. She let the breath she'd been holding escape from between her lips and the knot of tension in her stomach eased slightly. The air smelled slightly of cleaning fluid. *So far, so good.*

Arriving at the lift doors, she called for the lift. She glanced right, then left, and saw crewmembers appearing on adjoining corridors but they paid her no attention. The lift doors opened and she stepped inside. The doors closed and she was alone. "Deck seven," she said and the lift began to move. Thankfully it didn't require an access code to operate or the trip would have been a short one.

This seemed way too easy, especially considering she had just killed someone who seemed to fit the description of Stormcrow himself.

The lift doors slide open when the car stopped on deck seven. Once again the corridor appeared deserted beyond the doors. Steeling herself, Siren stepped out when a familiar voice made her heart seem to freeze in her chest.

"Well, well, this must be our rescuer."

Siren turned toward the voice coming from her right and her eyes went wide when she saw who was speaking. *Bones?*

Her massive friend stood with a plasma rifle aimed at her and a lopsided grin on his unshaven features. There was a fresh, jagged scar running across the middle of his forehead.

Beside him stood Gears, a blaster pistol in his right hand looking pale and thin. He seemed about to collapse. His right optical implant was absent, leaving a rim of red and angry flesh where the eye socket was, as if the implant had been forcefully removed.

"Aren't you two in prison?" Siren said.

Bones chuckled and lifted the barrel of the rifle to rest the butt on his right hip. Gears stuffed the blaster pistol in a holster hanging off his narrower-than-usual hips. "Good to see you, too," he said. "Are you here to rescue us?" He arched one eyebrow. Both men reeked of stale sweat and fried foods.

A smile drifted across Siren's lips. "Amongst other things, yes." She dropped her hand from the butt of her pistol. "Where are Stacks and Clobe?"

The grin on Bones' face dropped away and his eyes became hard. "They didn't make it. Long story. I'll tell ya later."

Nodding as she glanced to her left, then to her right, she asked, "Any welcome parties nearby?"

"Nope. Gears and I took care of the guards. My rifle's almost out of juice and his blaster is low on energy. We don't have any spare cartridges."

Bones' brow wrinkled. "Say, Siren, did you shoot a tall, dark, and mysterious guy dressed in all black?"

Looking around, Siren found the local SIN comm interface. "Yeah, Why?"

Bones grunted. "I killed two of 'em during our escape."

Siren shifted her gaze to Bones, expecting a wide grin, but she saw he was serious. "Clones?"

The big man nodded, his lips forming a grim line.

She shook her head. There would time later to deal with this issue. *I hope.* "SIN, where is the ANSS *Lightning*?"

Before the AI could reply, Bones said, "It's on hangar deck three. It's about—"

Gears interrupted. "Five hundred meters from our current location are fifty-seven enemy troopers, all heavily armed, and probably alerted by now to our escape from the cells."

Bones glanced at Gears, then looked back at Siren. Seeing the tech genius had stopped talking, he continued, "They'll be expecting us to try to make it back to our ship."

Siren arched an eyebrow at him. "Then we'll need a distraction."

15

BEHIND SIREN, BONES and Gears waited for her to activate the explosive devices she had attached to the shield generators and the portside weapons operational systems. She had also sent an encoded message to the *Thunder* to let them know the exact moment to attack the *Dark Storm*.

A tiny orange light blinked steadily on her comm, receiving the signals from the bombs as it counted down the exact second she should set off the explosives. The mini-bombs were powerful enough to destroy the generators and the blaster cannon controls. Her eyes were focused on the orange repeating glow until it suddenly changed to a steady purple.

She took in a deep breath before she tapped the "activate" icon on the screen of her handheld comm.

No sounds met Siren's hearing but she did feel a shiver from the deck under her feet.

Then the walls around them began to tremble and some of the ceiling tiles fell around them like rain. The *Thunder* had launched its full-scale attack right on cue, just as she activated the bombs. "Gears, we good?" The tech genius had a handheld scanner. He looked up from the readouts and nodded.

They had been in the corridor outside the hangar deck waiting for the moment to enter and retake the *Lightning*. The doors slid open as the deck under them heaved, nearly throwing Siren off balance but she, Gears, and Bones managed to remain upright since they'd been expecting the explosions. They raced through the open doors, weapons at the ready.

The guards that remained were either sprawled facedown, some in pools of blood, or had dropped their weapons and were bracing themselves against walls or hangar loading bots. Siren could see large launch pods lining the walls on both sides containing ships of various sizes and configurations. None appeared to be the *Lightning*.

She turned to face Bones. "Where is the ship?"

Bones tilted his head to his left as he lowered his rifle. She looked at him quizzically. His eyes flitted to her right, then back. She shifted her gaze to her right to see a cadre of six troopers in full battle armor, their plasma rifles leveled at them.

Stormcrow, with an amused smile on his lips, stood in the middle of the line of troopers.

It appears this mission is not going to end well, at least for Blaster Squad, thought Siren.

"You looking for your ship?" asked Stormcrow, his tone heavy with sarcasm.

Siren holstered her blaster and placed her hands on her hips; her features shifted to annoyance. "Stormcrow—or should I say Percy?— you are one piece of work. How did you survive? I shot you dead in the materializer chamber."

Stormcrow's eyes narrowed and his lips pursed. His cheeks flushed rust-red. She'd gotten him mad. It felt good.

His eyes hardened and his right hand dropped to a sheath on his left hip. He pulled a thin-bladed knife that gleamed in the light. The troopers had shifted the barrels of their rifles toward her as she insulted their leader but Stormcrow waved them away. They lowered their weapons and stepped back to increase the space between Blaster Squad and themselves.

Siren smirked dismissively. After unhooking her gun belt, she handed it to Bones, who glared at the mercenary leader.

Without a word, she took a step closer to Stormcrow, who visibly tensed.

His eyes remained hard and focused, his jawline set in determination. She could smell the musky sweat on him. Her hands were clenched in fists at her sides.

Stormcrow made the first move, quickly bringing up the knife and making a lunge at her chest, the blade flashing as it came at her. She sidestepped the mercenary leader and he passed her, missing her right arm by millimeters. She snapped a punch directly at the elbow of the arm holding the knife and he screamed in agony as the bones broke. The knife fell to the deck with a clatter and he bent forward, stumbling until he dropped to his knees holding his left arm, hanging limp at his side.

The troopers moved as one across the deck toward their fallen leader. Bones and Gears intercepted them, each wresting a plasma rifle from a startled trooper. They fired wildly and immediately two troopers disappeared in the fiery blaze of energy that enveloped them. Gears and Bones dropped to a crouch and fired at the remaining four troopers. They responded too slowly to their comrades' sudden disappearance and were immediately caught in the crossfire. They too disappeared in a flash of super-heated energy before they could return fire.

Siren lay on her side on the deck, a bloody gash in her side where a plasma beam had grazed her during the shootout. Searing pain forced her to grit her teeth. Though the pain clouded her mind, she heard two familiar voices that seemed far away. They sounded frantic and panicked. The acrid smell of blood filled her nose and mouth as she sucked in air.

The fog in her head slowly began to dissipate and the raised voices of her friends finally broke through, accompanied by the worst headache she had ever experienced. "Siren. I'll patch you up," shouted Bones as he swung his rifle attached to the strap around his bulky frame around to his back. He knelt next to her as he pulled out a spray-on field bandage, which he aimed at the wound in her side and sprayed a copious amount of the sealer. It coated the wound and the bleeding stopped but the wound pulsed, sending waves of pain through her body.

Gears stood nearby, his blaster at the ready, his one optical implant scanning for threats.

"SIN," said Bones. "Patch me through to the *Thunder*."

The response came immediately. "Go ahead." Siren's heart skipped a beat. It was Nick.

"Nick," she said softly. Her mouth was dry and she seemed to be floating on a cloud.

"Easy," Bones said, gently this time. "Nick, Siren's badly wounded. Transport her to sick bay. Gears and I will take the *Lightning*. We'll rendezvous in orbit."

"Acknowledged, Bones, but you better move fast. Our scans show Stormcrow's techs are making quick repairs to their systems, including their portside cannons."

A deep, ominous voice made them freeze where they were. "You bastards aren't going anywhere." Siren glanced to her left and saw Stormcrow standing with the by now familiar arrogant sneer on his stubble-covered face, his left arm hanging limply at his side. In the other hand he held a blaster.

"I should have killed you all when—" He suddenly stiffened and his eyes widened. In the center of where his chest should have been was a large, smoking hole through which she could see the expansive hangar behind him. His dead fingers let go of the blaster and it dropped to the deck, landing with a loud bang. He sagged and collapsed to the deck where he lay on his back, unmoving, his unseeing eyes still open.

"Shut up, you pompous jerk," Siren said, her voice harsh with the pain.

Her weapon now slipped from her fingers to land beside her body on the deck with a clatter, then she sagged back with a shudder of pure relief from the strain of having to fire the blaster from a partially sitting position. The warm trickle of blood seeping from the edges of the spray-on dressing was a welcome distraction.

The next thing Siren felt was the welcome tingle of a materializer beam enveloping her. The hangar around her began to fade until it finally disappeared in a dark abyss as the beam took her.

16

NICK WATCHED SIREN'S eyes flutter open and forced a tight smile on his lips. There was no point in letting her think her condition was hopeless, at least immediately. SIN said there was a faint hope she'd survive in spite of the blood loss and the damage to her internal organs. Though not exactly using those words.

Siren coughed, so Nick offered her a drink of water through the dispenser hose next to her head, which rested on the pillow of the bio-bed. Without being asked, the SIN raised her to a sitting position. She accepted the narrow dispenser hose into her mouth, then greedily took in two long sips and sighed after releasing the dispenser tube from between her dry, cracked lips.

Nick's heart was in his throat as he reached out to take hold of her hand. Her skin was cool to the touch. "It'll be okay, Siren, I'm here," he whispered.

Siren's eyes focused as she turned and gazed into his. The look of sadness behind her eyes burned into his soul. "I killed Stormcrow," she whispered.

Nick nodded slightly. She may have killed another of the Stormcrow clones Gears told him about, but not the real thing. "You saved Bones and Gears." He paused to swallow a sob. "Like you always do."

Her hand gripped his tightly. "Don't lie to me, Nick, not now."

His brow wrinkled and his heart beat faster. "No, of course not…"

"I'm dying." Her lean frame was wracked by a soul-shattering cough, but she managed to maintain her grip on his hand. He nodded and his chin dropped to his chest as a single tear escaped his left eye to run down his cheek.

Her grip suddenly tightened, then slowly relaxed until her hand was limp in his. A rattle of air escaping her lungs, shook her lean frame as her last breath left her now lifeless body.

She was dead.

Nick gently placed her hand on her chest. Her eyes were closed and her flesh was pale, the color that remained now drained completely from her cheeks. Her expression was calm as if she were in a deep sleep.

It comforted him to think she was finally at peace.

"Captain." It was Gears calling him on the ships comm system.

He turned away from his friend and walked to the comm unit in the wall. Gathering his emotions, Nick tapped the activation button. "Yes, Gears, what's up?"

"The Admiral wants to talk to you."

"Okay, I'll be in my quarters in five minutes."

Nick paused and wiped his eyes with the back of one hand, then looked over his shoulder at the still form of his friend on the bio-bed. His stomach muscles tightened as a burst of anger welled up from deep inside him. He turned away and walked to a lift opposite the row of three bio-beds in the sick bay.

Soon he sat at his desk in the captain's quarters recently vacated by Siren and sucked in a deep breath before tapping the comm button next to the viewer terminal inset in the desk. He thought he could smell a trace of her distinctive odor of powdered rose petals as the viewer came on to reveal the grim features of Grand Admiral Bellot Schipp, who stood on the command deck of the dreadnought class command ship, ANSS *Colin Powell*.

The command ship headed a fleet of battlewagons, destroyers, and sixteen wings of single pilot attack vessels.

The Alliance fleet had arrived to blast Stormcrow's command ship to dust soon after Blaster Squad disabled the *Dark Shadow*. It didn't take long before mercenary ships within the system were either destroyed, captured, or fled the system.

Disturbingly, weapons expert Pieter Zoeks had also disappeared. There was some indication the real Stormcrow had escaped the destruction of his fleet, but this was yet to be confirmed. Nick was more worried about these two disappearances occurring simultaneously than about anything else. It suggested Zoeks was working for Stormcrow and possibly the Master. It certainly explained recent events if there had been a traitor aboard one of his ships.

"Any trace of Stormcrow?" the Admiral growled.

Nick fought the urge to snap back his reply. He really disliked this pompous ass. Instead he gritted his teeth. "No, sir. Nothing so far."

The Admiral's cheeks flushed a brilliant reddish hue. "It is imperative we locate that bastard." He turned away as if ignoring Nick. "You need to drive the men harder. You command the two fastest ships in the fleet and we need to find and capture this terrorist sooner than later. I want to try and execute him quickly and quietly."

Odd choice of word to describe his long-time competitor, thought Nick. *Terrorist?*

He'd known Percy Nicely for decades and he wouldn't classify him a terrorist. Sure, the mercenary leader was a ruthless killer and lacked moral fiber, and he took any job that paid well. Overthrowing legitimate governments, assassination, robbery, and other crimes, but terror had never been in his playbook. "Maybe he's changed," mused Nick under his breath.

The admiral spun sharply toward the viewer, his eyes filled with rage. "What did you say, Justice?"

"Nothing, sir, other than I will track him down quickly." He paused. "I can't guarantee he'll surrender." He intentionally arched both eyebrows to emphasis his next words before adding, "If you get my meaning, Admiral."

The Admiral grunted derisively and waved Nick away dismissively. "Just get it done." He glared at Nick through the viewer. "I expect results."

"I'll contact you when we have him in custody. Sir." Without waiting for a reply, Nick cut the connection.

The comm buzzed softly again. Nick sighed. Today had taken an almost unbearable emotional toll on him. "Yes."

"Sorry to bother you, sir, but we completed the review of the data we extracted from the *Dark Storm*'s AI before we escaped," said Gears.

Nick rubbed his eyes with the palms of his hands. He could feel a headache beginning at the base of his skull. "And?"

"We have the identity of the Master."

The headache suddenly disappeared. Nick leaned forward in his chair as a shot of excitement enveloped him. "Who?"

"The newest chairperson of the Alliance council, Lokfor Ust."

Nick froze. This made sense but made the defeat of the Master more complicated than ever. They had thought the Master was on the board, not the chairperson. It meant she murdered Whizzar and Grand Admiral Costello and was responsible for the death of his closest friend.

His eyes narrowed and a feeling of calm, controlled rage boiled up in him. They were going to pay, all of them, and pay dearly.

Nick cleared his throat. "SIN is the upload complete?"

"Yes, Captain."

A small smile played across Nick's lips ending at the corners of his eyes.

Look for the exciting conclusion to this adventure in Blaster Squad #7, The Empire Strikes.

About the Author

International selling Star Trek author, Russ Crossley, writes science fiction and fantasy, and mystery/suspense as well as their various subgenres.

His latest science fiction satire set in the far future, Revenge of the Lushites, is a sequel to Attack of the Lushites released in 2011. Both titles are available in e-book and trade paperback.

He has sold several short stories that have appeared in anthologies from various publishers including; WMG Publishing, Pocket Books, 53rd Street Publishing, and St. Martins Press.

He is a member of SF Canada and is past president of the Greater Vancouver Chapter of Romance Writers of America. He is also an alumni of the Oregon Coast Professional Fiction Writers Master Class taught by award winning author/editors, Kristine Katherine Rusch and Dean Wesley Smith.

Feel free to contact him on Facebook, Twitter, or his website http//:www.russcrossley.com. He loves to hear from readers.

Other titles by Russ Crossley you may enjoy

The Trudy Wilson Mystery Novel Series
Bad Loyalty
Shear Murder
Buzzcut - coming soon

Blaster Squad
#1 Terror on the Moon
#2 Sea of Death
#3 Planet of Doom
#4 Raiders of Cloud City
#5 Rise of the Empire

Other Novels

Attack of the Lushites
Revenge of the Lushites
My Zombie Prince
Antique Virgin
The Fire In Their Hearts
with R.S. Meger (from Champagne Books)
Zomopolis
The Last Serial Killer

Razor and Edge Mysteries
The Kidnapping of Billy Buttons
String of Pearls
Death by Clown
Beggin' For Murder
Ragged Ice
The Grand Central Mystery

A Strange Case of Undead Murder

Jazz Stiletto Mysteries
A Day Without Sunshine
Skullduggery
Instrument of justice (first published in Over My
Dead Body online mystery magazine)

The Amanda Dark paranormal mysteries
Hook Island
Grind Manor
Moonrise Diner
A Father's Daughter

Short Stories
Countdown
Shoeless Moe
Round Up At The Burger Bar:
The Story of Trixie Pug, Parts 1, 2, 3, 4, 5, 6, 7, 8, 9
Five Minutes
Blossom Queen, Barbarian
The Secret
The Family Line
End of the Flies
Death by Magic
The Penguin Sleeps With The Fishes
Only The Worthy
Hero For A Day
End of Empire
Strange Bedfellows
Big Business

A Perfect Crime
The Wise Guy and The Pirates
In Search of the Perfect Cup
T.I.N. Men
The Legend of G and the Dragonettes
The Incredible Mr. Fix-It
Lock Stock and Barrel
Divided Loyalties
Cave of Wonders
A Family Empire
Until We Meet Again
Dragon Rising
Solitary Man
The Keel Mountain Conspiracy
Angel on My Shoulder
Heroes of Old
The Great Bicycle Race
Tikka's Big Day
"My Partner the Zombie" —
Hungry For Your Love Anthology
(St. Martin's Press)
Big Hairy Deal
One Red Shoe
A Bad Day in Lunden Texas
Bloody Betty, Queen of the Pirates
Mirror Image
Dangerous Waters
Cape Disappointment
Boomerang
The Watcher of Wayburn Street
The Apprentice
Drip!

A Beautiful Friendship and The Parrot of Doom
Robine's Diary
The Christmas Club
Loose Ends
Splatter Pattern
It Takes Two
Lexicon
Replacement Parts
Sidekicks
Lost Stories
Time and Space
Survivors
Neighborhood Watch
Unnatural Immortal
Rum Runner's Lounge
It's A Small Galaxy
A Shattered Man
Betrayed
Replacement Parts
Clubhouse Heroes
Sounds That Angels Make
Muggins Rules – originally published in Fiction River
Volume 12, Risk Takers

Anthologies
Tales of Urban Fantasy
Five Tales of Bizarre Detectives
Tales of Mystery and Suspense
Tales of Weird Fantasy
Tales of Twisted Crime
Tales of The Unexpected
Tales From Space

10 by Russ Crossley
Round Up At The Burger Bar: The Story of Trixie Pug,
Parts 1- 5 The Beginning
Worlds of Science Fiction and Fantasy
More Tales of Mystery and Suspense
Justice Served
Love Stories
Ladies of the Jolly Roger with Rita Schulz
The Adventures of Razor and Edge:
Five Tales From The Quirky Detective Team
An Unexpected Journey
On Edge
Thrilling Adventures
Total War
Courageous

Non-Fiction
The Writers Tools - The Synopsis

Also available from 53rd Street Publishing
http://www.53rdstreetpublishing.com

See how it all started and meet Blaster Squad for the
first time.

In the 42nd century alien pirates steal a deadly virus
threatening to wipe out billions of lives. A team of
highly trained mercenaries known as Blaster Squad
springs into action to stop the pirates deadly plot and
save the galaxy from certain doom.

Blaze across the galaxy with Star Trek author Russ
Crossley and a new brand of mercenaries who are
willing to break all the rules to win.